D1276022

KNIGHTS' RANSOM

Young Vahl Thorfinnsson, falconer to the son of the Duke of Burgundy, accompanies his master on a crusade against the Turks. The expedition ends in disaster, and Vahl's master and many other noble knights are held prisoner by the Turks until they can be ransomed.

One part of the ransom is practically impossible to obtain. The Turkish Sultan demands twelve Greenland falcons — huge, fierce white birds that must be captured in far-off Greenland.

Vahl and a companion undertake the perilous quest to secure the falcons, encountering many obstacles and dangers, too, as pirates seek to capture and icebergs threaten to destroy their frail ship.

Here is a story for every young person who enjoys tales of mystery and adventure. Authentic historical background.

S. F. WELTY

KNIGHTS' RANSOM

√W4685k

WILCOX & FOLLETT Co. CHICAGO

New York   Toronto

Glossary

BATE — *to beat the wings impatiently, or spring up in a flutter from the fist or block. (Said of falcons.)*

BLOCK — *the wooden perch on which a falcon is kept*

BOUND — *said of a falcon which has seized its prey in mid-air and clung to it*

CADGER — *the carrier of the cadge — the wooden circular frame on which hawks are carried to the field*

CAST — *to throw up the indigestible remains, bones, feathers, etc., following the bird's meal*

CONDOTTIERE — *a captain of a roving band of mercenary soldiers*

COTE-HARDIE — *a close-fitting tunic with sleeves and, usually, a belt*

CREANCE — *a line fastened to the leash of a hawk*

EYAS — *a hawk captured while still a nestling*

GLEBE — *the land belonging, or yielding revenue, to the church*

GOSHAWK — *a short-winged falcon*

HACK — *a state of partial liberty in which young untrained falcons are kept*

HAGGARD — *a hawk which was captured after reaching adulthood*

JESSES — *leather strips worn on the hawk's legs*

JUPON — *a quilted doublet or tunic*

LEASH — *a leather thong fastened to the jesses of the falcon*

LURE — *a dead bird, or a bunch of feathers and raw meat, used to recall falcons from their flight*

MEWS — *a stable for falcons*

MISERICORDE — *a thin-bladed medieval dagger*

PEREGRINE FALCON — *a swift, courageous long-winged falcon found almost everywhere in the world*

REBEC — *a stringed musical instrument*

SCAPULARY — *a monk's sleeveless outer garment, which falls from the shoulders*

SKERRIES — *rocky isles or reefs*

SWIVELS — *small rings through which the leash of a falcon is attached to the jesses, in order to secure the bird*

TIERCEL — *a male hawk (The largest and fiercest falcons are females.)*

TRIVET — *a metal plate on very short legs, used under a hot dish to protect the table*

VERJUICE — *an acid liquor made from the sour juice of crab apples, unripe grapes, apples, etc.*

WEATHER — *to be tethered unhooded in the open air (Said of falcons)*

WELL-MANNED — *well tamed, and accustomed to strangers (Said of falcons)*

I

Crusader

VAHL THORFINNSSON, young falconer to Count John of Nevers, sat his restless horse on the edge of the army waiting for the Archbishop's blessing. A scarlet lure tufted with white feathers swung from his saddle. Crusader, his master's Greenland falcon, perched on his gauntletted fist. The great white bird, with white-plumed hood and jesses of scarlet leather, and silver Indian bells on its feet, attracted stares and comments from the peasant folk of Paris as they crowded by up the hill.

"Don't push me near that fierce bird!"

"I hope that hawk never chases my pigeons!"

"But what good will it be fighting the Turks?"

Vahl smiled to himself. Pride filled him. Even ignorant peasants could see that Crusader was a rare bird! Every French nobleman kept hunting hawks according to his rank, but no lesser man than a prince could own a bird like this. In all France there were only three Greenland falcons; and he, Vahl Thorfinnsson, was in charge of one of them!

The chatter of the peasants around Vahl faded. They shrank back to make room as Duke Philip of Burgundy himself led his retinue up the hill toward the wooden dais which had been built on its crest. The Duke's sharp eyes caught sight of the bird and he reined in his horse.

"Guard that falcon well, lad. She is worth a king's ransom."

"I shall do my best, Lord Philip," Vahl avowed. He knew that Philip of Burgundy thought his son John a fool to trust such a treasure to a boy of sixteen, but Vahl meant to prove him wrong.

The Duke lifted his hand in acknowledgement of Vahl's words and rode on.

When Vahl turned in his saddle, his keen blue eyes could see the whole scene spread out on the gentle slope of Montmartre. Behind, the city wall of Paris unwound like a brown ribbon on the green earth. A living wall of the people of Paris encircled the crusaders as they faced the dais where the Princes of the Fleur-de-lis were gathering, waiting for the Prince of the Church.

The whole grassy plain was suddenly blooming with flowers of silk and steel. The plate armor of the knights reflected the warm spring sunshine

8

from a thousand polished surfaces. Each rider sat his horse with his bridle in his right hand and his helmet in his left. Beside each stood his squire, holding the knight's shield and lance. Squires and men-at-arms in their tunics of stuffed leather, with hoods, mantles, and hose of dark green, wine, brown, or black wool, set off by contrast the gorgeous hues of their masters' scarlet, yellow, and purple jupons, and the jewelled bridles and plumed crests of the horses. Pennons high on lance tips fluttered in the March breeze. Thousands of knights were there, and more were gathering.

"A handsome bird," said a deep, faintly accented voice behind Vahl, so close to his ear that he was startled. A small and swarthy stranger in rich black garb of foreign cut had ridden close. His jewelled hand reached out toward the hawk.

"Not too close, my lord!" Vahl cried quickly.

"Think you a touch would harm the bird?" asked the knight sarcastically.

"Nay, messire," Vahl answered earnestly. "But if the falcon raked you with her sharp claws, the wound might go deep, and I would be responsible."

"I need no lessons in falconry, varlet!" snapped the knight. "Hand me the bird. I would but carry it a short while."

"I dare not, my lord. Count John has forbidden me to let anyone but himself touch it without his order."

9

"Doubtless he would have you drawn and quartered if you disobeyed," sneered the courtier.

"I do not mean to test him," said Vahl, a little grimly. John of Nevers was known for his hasty temper.

"Pish! Such an order is only for yokels! I but wish to compare the bird with my master's. Hand it to me without more ado."

He held out his gloved fist. Vahl said sturdily, "I am sorry, my lord —"

"You defy me, do you?" His black brows drew together. "Learn to obey your betters, you fool!" He rose in his stirrups and struck Vahl full in the face. Blinded momentarily, the boy instinctively lifted his arm against another blow. The huge bird on his fist suddenly bated. Her wide wings flapped, the bells on her legs tinkled, and her cruel beak snapped almost in the eye of the stranger's horse. The beast reared up in terror. The knight clutched wildly at the air and fell to the ground. The bird bated again; the frantic horse bolted. Nearby peasants set up a shout and snatched at its bridle, but it charged off down the hill, scattering those in its path. Hearing the commotion, a knight and squire gave chase, and brought back the steed.

They found Vahl dismounted, Crusader still on his fist, trying to give his free hand to help up the fallen man.

"Keep your hands off me!" the knight snarled,

his dark face red with humiliation. "I want no help from a churl!" He got to his feet, snatched his horse's bridle from the knight who had brought it, and mounted. "I shall not forget the insult you have put on me!" he growled to Vahl, and rode off.

"What exquisite manners! How courteous were the thanks of my old acquaintance!" remarked the knight who had returned the horse, with mock admiration. "What brought on his rage, young falconer?"

"I would not allow him to take the falcon."

"Rightly," nodded the knight. "That weal on your face is a mark of honor. But he will not love you hereafter. I hope for your sake he does not go on the crusade."

He rode off with his young companion. Vahl stared after the strangers, but they made their way through the crowd straight into the company of the leaders. It was easy for his eyes to follow their flowing mantles of garnet velvet, each with the same crest — a golden lyre encircled by a crown. They took their places close beneath the gold-embroidered white banner of the Virgin Mary, which fluttered in the place of honor next to John of Nevers' pennon. But it was the strange objects hanging at their backs which roused Vahl's wonder. A young Burgundian squire rode up near Vahl, and the boy asked him,

"Look, Paul! Can those be minstrels?"

Paul craned his neck for a better view.

"Minstrels? Going on this crusade? What a crazy — why, God be praised, they are minstrels! It is Sir Olivier of Artois and his son! I did not know they answered the Duke's call for men. The Turks had best flee if they ever meet Sir Olivier!"

"A weakling harp-player? I could fell him with one blow of my fist," sneered a burly groom, who had taken his place nearby with several pack horses.

Paul grinned. "Maybe you could if you caught him blindfolded from behind! Even then you had best say your prayers first. Only the Devil would hear them afterward."

"Is he really such a fighter?" asked the groom, doubtful but half-impressed.

"He led a Free Company in his youth, and won wealth and honor as one of the greatest captains in Italy," Paul explained. "But hush! There comes the Archbishop."

Vahl looked quickly toward the dais. Philip of Burgundy stood there with his Duchess behind him and John of Nevers' wife at her side. There was the half-mad king, Charles VI, sane enough today, apparently, for he stood straight and regal in his jewelled robes of state. The beautiful young woman on his right, Vahl knew, was the Duchess Valentina, the Duke of Orleans' Italian wife. Her husband, who was the king's brother, gave his unwavering attention as usual to blonde Queen Isabeau.

In his purple and scarlet robes, the Archbishop
approached the platform where the royalty of France
awaited him. The procession was led by chanting
priests, clad in black and white, with a great cross
carried before them. As the Archbishop mounted
the steps, the crowd bent like grass in the wind.
The proud nobles, many of whom bent their knees
to no man but their king, and sometimes defied
even him, bared and bowed their heads to God.
Beside each knelt his squire, and around them all,
the people of Paris bowed to the ground.

"God will bless you!" the Archbishop cried.
"His curse will fall upon that impious Turkish
sultan who has boasted that he will conquer Rome
and feed oats to his horse upon the altar of Saint
Peter! Go now, soldiers of the Cross! Save, serve,
and increase the Kingdom of God!"

"We go! We go!" cried the knights with one
voice, amid a sudden clank and clatter of armor.
A few voices began a new shout; it was taken up
here and there, then by the whole multitude, crusaders and watching townsfolk alike. It echoed and
re-echoed over the field: "On! On to Jerusalem!"

That was the farewell of the thousand foremost
knights of France and their retainers, as they set
forth from Paris toward the kingdom of Hungary.
There King Sigismond waited to lead them against
the invading Turkish sultan, Bajazet.

The great crusades had long since died out of

the Holy Land. The conquering Christians had been conquered in their turn and driven out by the Turks. Now again infidels threatened to march into the Christian lands of Europe. At the call of Pope Boniface the Ninth from Rome, staunch sons of the Church were setting out from all central Europe to do battle for their God.

As the leaders of the French cavalcade began at last to move, women and children broke in among the ranks of the crusaders to claim last kisses before their men marched away. A thin and scraggly woman with two chubby little girls rushed up to the burly groom and clung to him, weeping bitterly, until Vahl felt the tears come into his own eyes. But it was the folk left behind he felt sorry for; he himself longed for the adventures of the crusade.

It was some time before the baggage train with which he was to ride began to move. Vahl let his horse browse on the short grass, while the people nearby streamed slowly back to their homes in the city. They blessed him and his companions as they passed. Amid their chatter Vahl suddenly heard a young woman's voice say clearly:

"Here is Count John's Greenland falcon! Is she well-manned, boy?"

Vahl turned in his saddle and found himself facing Queen Isabeau and the Duchess of Orleans. Doffing his cap, he bent deeply.

"She is becoming so, my lady."

"So, we hope, is Charles' bird," said the Queen. Duke Philip of Burgundy, Count John of Nevers, and King Charles had bought the rare hawks only a few months before from the falcon fair at Valkenswaard in Brabant, and their falconers had vied in trying to train them. "Charles is looking forward to rare sport."

"He should have it," the Duchess declared. "My father paid a fortune for his birds, but he says they would be cheap at any price."

"Greenland falcons?" asked Isabeau incredulously. "I thought none but these three had been brought to Europe for years."

"I doubt if many have," said the beautiful Italian. "My father got only two and considered himself lucky. Some Italian seamen who had been adventuring with Jarl Sinclair of the Orkneys brought them back from the north, along with several darker falcons from Iceland."

Paying no more attention to the interested young falconer, the ladies rode on, their maids and courtiers following in their train. Among the last riders Vahl saw the swarthy Italian in black velvet; hastily he turned his horse and hoped he would go unnoticed. Luck was with him for the knight was deep in conversation with a French courtier and looked neither left nor right. Vahl caught a scrap of their talk as they went by.

"Now I can take ship with an easy heart," said

the foreigner. "My lord's kingdom will be safe from attack."

"For a time, at least," replied the Frenchman. "For which his daughter will thank God! John of Nevers would rather have fought against him than against the Turks!"

Their voices faded as they rode off. Vahl sighed with relief as he looked after them. Praise be to God, that Italian was not going on the crusade! From what Vahl had heard, he must have come from Milan, where ruled the father of Valentina of Orleans. Vahl remembered rumors, before the crusade was decided upon, that John of Nevers was begging his father to let him march south and conquer the rich duchy of Milan. Evidently the Duke of Milan had heard those stories too. . . . But there was no time to speculate; the ten companies were at last on the march.

Count John, at the head of the foremost company, led the way slowly toward the highway east. With him rode a hundred of the great knights of Burgundy. Behind them came the mounted lancers and bowmen, and after these the baggage train, with its pack horses and mules in charge of trusted squires.

In this train Vahl rode next to Father Bernard, chaplain to John of Nevers. The priest was charged not only with the welfare of the company's souls, but with their bodily care as well. Since he was a physician, his pack mules bore the portable altar, the holy water and holy oil, the rosaries and medals needful to his office, and also the ointments and herbs for wounded bodies. Vahl was in charge of two mules, which carried a palanquin for Count John's falcons and gear for hawking. All the boy's own baggage he carried upon his horse's back, behind his saddle.

For a few hours the other companies rode close on the heels of the Burgundians, but as the day wore on they stretched farther apart. When he turned, Vahl could see them at a great distance, spread out in a straggling line.

In the eight years since Thorfinn had brought his motherless son from Norway to the Burgundian court, Vahl had seldom been more than a day's journey distant from the courtyard of the Hôtel d'Artois. But he had hunted so often around the city that he knew every landmark. He was still on familiar ground when the army camped that night.

The common soldiers built huge bonfires over which they could cook their porridge; the squires pitched the tents of their knight commanders. The pavilions turned a grassy pasture into a bed of huge mushrooms, striped in bright red and blue. A giant picnic party could have been no more free from care.

Munching bread and cheese, Vahl let his mules graze near him on the grass while his unhooded birds weathered on their blocks. Tired and a bit sleepy, he was suddenly startled to hear a young voice say close behind him:

"Look, Father! Here is Count John's Greenland falcon. This time let us look at it closely."

Vahl leaped up, turning. The minstrel knight and squire, still clothed alike in garnet velvet, were walking toward Crusader. Sir Olivier carried a golden harp in hands gauntletted in garnet velvet, his gloves alone distinguishing his garb from his son's. The boy, a little younger than Vahl, carried a rebec, but his bare right hand reached toward the falcon.

"Look all you like, messires," said Vahl hastily. "But I pray you, do not touch the bird. Count John forbids it."

"Greetings, young falconer!" said the knight, smiling. "We will not quarrel with you like that knight this morning!"

"Father," said the youthful squire, "you should be a prince, so that I could fly such a bird as this. Is it not rare sport, falconer?"

"Count John thinks so," Vahl agreed, grinning. "He refused to lead this crusade until his father tempted him by a gift of this bird!"

"How is it," asked the knight, "that he trusts such a prize to a young lad like you?"

"I have worked with hawks all my life," Vahl explained. "My father was chief falconer to Duke Philip of Burgundy, and I was his cadger. When he died last winter, Duke Philip gave his place to his assistant, and I was no more wanted at the Hôtel d'Artois. But Duke John knew I had helped my father train this falcon, and he gave me charge of all his birds."

"Was the hawk hard to train?" asked Sir Olivier.

"Much easier than we expected," Vahl told him. "She was an eyas that had been kept at hack and broken to the hood before she was ever sold at Valkenswaard. I know not who trained her, but he was a master. Because she was wild and fierce, we tried her first with leash and creance, but soon found she did not need them. She was trained to both lure and fist in a few weeks, but it was full two months before she was well-manned. Since then she is a hunter any prince might love to sport with."

"Could you not promise to oversleep some morning?" asked the squire, his eyes twinkling. "I think I shall come some night and steal this treasure from you — just for long enough to fly her at one heron!"

"Nay," Vahl said, mock-seriously. "I hear the very blades of grass growing in the night! Besides, you know the story of the squire who flew the King of Norway's falcon without his consent."

"I never heard it. Tell it," commanded the boy eagerly.

"The falcon took a heron. The foolish squire

boasted. The king vowed that in punishment the squire should eat that heron from its feathers to its feet. He was choked to death."

"That would make a good ballad," said Sir Olivier.

"So it would!" agreed his son. "Thanks, falconer. We need a new lay. But some day I am going to fly that bird there, with Count John's consent. Mark me!"

"*I* mark you!" laughed his father. "If ever you earn Count John's favor so far, Artur, I will give you these embroidered gloves you are always hounding me for — if they are not long since worn out!"

"Witness that promise, falconer!" Artur begged. "And laugh all you like, Father. I'll wager I get those gloves some day."

They passed on toward Count John's tent. Vahl was exhausted by the day's excitement. He tethered his mules to a tree and made his six birds safe in their palanquin. Then he lay down beside them in his leathern sleeping bag, with a ribald camp song for a lullaby. Afterward he thought he heard another song, sung far off in a magnificent strong bass, in which he caught only the words "Norway" and "falcon." But when he woke at the first hint of light in the sky, he thought perhaps he had dreamed it.

It would be an hour before the camp stirred. Vahl peeped at his birds; luckily a peregrine falcon had already cast. He whispered to Father Bernard to guard the palanquin, took the hawk, and rode quickly to the nearest field. Luck was with him. The peregrine took a rabbit and a partridge in quick succession. Vahl called the bird to him with his swinging lure, and retrieved the game. At least his charges would not starve on their first day of crusading.

That day the land began to grow strange to Vahl. For the most part, the company followed an old Roman road. Its stone paving had long since been broken and grown over with grass, but it still furnished solid footing. It led gradually upward to the east, out of the gently rolling plains of the Paris basin, to high and higher hills.

The country was thickly peopled, yet the towns and villages were only islands in a great sea of wild woodland. Vahl liked to come to a town, even though the army encamped outside the walls. A town meant feasting, and singing and dancing in the streets, or perhaps a market fair; and certainly High Mass in the cathedral before the march went on.

Vahl enjoyed, too, bartering with the peasant women in their coarse homespun smocks for fresh bread and cheese, or meat and verjuice, to add to the beans and meal porridge which were the common fare on the road. He waved at the weary serfs, plodding behind the wooden plows drawn by their yoked oxen up and down the long narrow strips of land assigned to them to till. After cultivating a third of the best village land for the lord of the manor, and a third of the next best for the glebe so that the priest and the Church would be well cared for, it was hard work for the peasants to scratch a living from their own few poor acres.

The leaders of the crusade stopped often at the manor houses. They bought provisions for their men and mounts from the storage barns beside the manor mill, had their horses new-shod and equipment mended at the smithy, and dined in state in the great hall. Thus they passed their time in holiday spirits, leaving the Isle of France behind, crossing the duchy of Burgundy into the counties of Bar and Lorraine, then traversing Alsace.

In Germany the Emperor had commanded that every road should be open to them. The grim castles on the heights overlooking the valley passes let down their drawbridges and welcomed the marchers in. From each castle, picked German nobles rode as guides on the eastward way.

Vahl rode companionably with the other squires or beside the priest, in the baggage train. Father Bernard looked severe in the black mantle which almost hid his white tunic and white scapulary, but under the black hood which covered his tonsured head, his brown-bearded face was kind. He loved to talk of the lands through which they rode. He had wandered through them as a young Dominican Friar on a preaching mission, and still remembered some of the dialect of the people. When the army encamped, his talk gathered a score of gawking peasants around him; and when he rode on, the faces he left behind were friendly.

In the evenings the priest ministered to sick bodies with his medicines, and to sick souls with the confessional; and then Vahl found himself lonely. His guardianship of the hawks kept him from joining the sports of the other young squires. When there was light enough for the birds to work with the lure, he kept them busy until dark.

Many another knight than Count John had brought his favorite hawk with him; and in company with them John of Nevers often rode with a bird on his fist, enjoying sport by the way. To keep the Count's six birds always in health, however, taxed Vahl's ingenuity. They needed fresh food every day. Their daily exercise involved much extra riding. Sometimes he could slip away to one side of the main body of the column, and work with the falcons while the horsemen waited for the slower baggage train to overtake them. But this did not give him sufficient time for all the birds. He decided to rise early each morning, and to fly one or two before the march began.

Accordingly, one dawn, he rode westward along the winding path which the crusaders had followed the day before. The country was hilly, wooded, and wild. Only a few poor charcoal burners' huts, with swine rooting near them under the trees, marked it as inhabited.

Vahl reasoned that to go ahead of the line of march might lose him from his companions. Going back, he would be between the Burgundian company and the nearest division of the army behind it. Even if he delayed too long, and was left behind by his own group, he would still be among friends.

He soon found a little valley near a turn in the road where the woods on each side were separated by an open field. He became so engrossed in flying Crusader that the sun was well above the horizon before he called the bird back to his fist. He was fastening on the plumed hood, when he thought he heard a faint scream. He listened intently; it seemed to him that he heard other voices, but he could see no one. He drew back into the shadow of a spreading oak, leashed the falcon on a branch as high as he could reach, and put his hand on his sword.

Shrill, piercing, closer, a woman's voice screamed again. Through the woods near him crashed three burly bearded peasants, dragging with them two resisting women. In the distance, another man's voice shouted after them.

Sword in hand, Vahl galloped toward them, crying, "What is this?" The foremost man yelled at him in a strange tongue, not slackening his pace or loosening his grip on the young woman he jerked after him, but threatening Vahl with the huge wooden staff he carried. The older woman tore her arm from her captor's grasp and ran forward, shrieking, holding out her hands. But the second man seized her and pulled her violently back, while the third man dealt her a cruel blow on the mouth. Vahl waited for no further answer; he attacked.

Mounted though he was, the peasants had him at a disadvantage. Their staves were stout, with a longer reach than that of Vahl's sword. Unhindered by the women, they would have made short work of him. But the young girl, released as her abductor leaped aside to ward off Vahl's blow, rushed at the second man with teeth and nails, while the older dame likewise bit and scratched with all her strength. Vahl succeeded in turning aside the blows of his first enemy and beat down his assailant's staff, wounding the man deeply in the side. But the women were able to win Vahl only a reprieve; they were struck down and lay moaning. Vahl saw both the other men come at him, teeth bared viciously like those of wild boars. He wheeled his horse so that he could, at least for an instant, keep one man behind the other. Then shouting "God and Right!" he charged forward again.

"God and Right!" sounded an echo. He could not look to see where it came from, for he was fighting for his life. But another horseman rushed into the fray beside him, and drew off one enemy. Against the other Vahl renewed his furious lunges, but it was the man's own bad luck which finished him. He tripped over a tree root, and fell sprawling. Vahl leaped down and stood over his prostrate body until the young woman, collecting her wits, bound his hands tightly behind him with her girdle, and tied his feet together with the wide linen band which formed her white cap. Then, picking up the fallen man's staff, Vahl ran to the aid of his hard-pressed rescuer.

Attack from two sides was too much for the peasant. He was soon beaten to his knees, and the older woman's girdle put to use to bind him.

As Vahl leaned panting on the staff he had seized, he looked squarely at his companion for the first time. It was Artur, the squire who had vowed to fly Crusader! But he was dressed now in plain wool and leather. Ambling toward them from the road came a French knight carrying his hawk. It was Artur's father, Sir Olivier the minstrel.

"That was a merry fight," Sir Olivier called casually. "What started it?"

"I know not," Vahl answered. "I do not speak their tongue." He blushed, for the two women had crawled to his feet and were kissing his hands, babbling what to his ears was jargon.

Sir Olivier, however, began speaking to them

in the same guttural language, and their faces lighted with joy as they saw themselves understood.

"They say," Artur translated rapidly to Vahl, "that this wounded knave you dispatched before I came demanded the girl in marriage. When her father and mother refused him, since he was known to be lawless, and they are honest people, though only poor charcoal burners, he vowed that he would take both the girl and revenge for their insult. To-day he came with his friends — what is that?"

Crackling underbrush nearby sent the young men's hands to their swords again. But the bloody-pated man who limped toward them was unarmed except for a knife. He was hardly in sight before the women were at his side, pointing excitedly to their fallen enemies and to their rescuers. The man stared, with fierce black eyes; then, with a vicious kick at one of his prostrate foes, he came forward, knelt at Sir Olivier's feet, and poured out a torrent of words. Sir Olivier answered with authority.

"Father is saying that our division of the French army will pass by in a few moments," Artur explained. "They will do justice to the miscreants." The man to whom his father spoke bowed.

"We ride ahead of our company with a message for Count John," Sir Olivier said, as Vahl mounted. "We will go with you."

Vahl answered, "Let me but reclaim the bird, and I am ready."

2

Ambush

N A SUNNY DAY in April, the French army came at last in sight of the city of Buda on the Danube with the king's castle towering above it. Sigismond and his knights rode forth, with bugles blowing and kettledrums booming, to do honor to their guests. Then the Hungarians wheeled their horses and led the way through the valley toward the castle.

So many were the French knights and their retainers that the castle could not quarter them all, and they were scattered about in the town below. Indeed, when the allied armies from Germany, Bohemia, Austria, and Hungary gathered there a few weeks later, there was no room for them even in the city. They encamped around it like a great ring of besiegers. Before they left Buda, Vahl wondered if the poor Hungarians did not think they were truly besiegers. Their visit stretched out a long time. The people were heavily taxed to provide them with meat and drink and to store up provisions for their further march.

Vahl took care of his falcons and the beasts that carried them in a tiny corner of the stable in the castle's outer courtyard. This was just on one side of the great drawbridge, within the castle's outer wall. It was a favored spot, assigned to him because Lord John wanted his falcons near, and well-housed.

Vahl had the freedom of the whole courtyard. He found a wide stone bench where the birds could weather on their blocks, and there he sat among them or walked nearby with one hawk on his hand, watching all the passers-by. He saw the leaders of the gathering armies when they came in to the King's feasts or rode out to hunt by the river. The nobles were all falcon fanciers, and Crusader was a nine-days wonder. Most of the men knew Greenland falcons by hearsay but had never seen any. Knights often stopped to speak to Vahl, who discovered that falconers' talk was about the same in any language.

Even Wenzel, the Emperor of Germany, and his younger brother Sigismond, King of Hungary and master of Buda, stopped one day. Wenzel was slow and sleepy-eyed, fat from overeating, and unsteady from too much wine. He spoke in thick German gutturals, and Vahl had to guess at his words from some similarity to his own Norse tongue. Sigismond took pity on Vahl's confusion and spoke to him in French. The King was in his thirties, with fair hair and a fine figure which made him look younger. Restless and active though he was, he enjoyed learning. Besides French and German, he spoke Latin, Bohemian, and Italian; and when he found that Vahl could speak Norwegian, he addressed him in a few words of that language. This produced mutual satisfaction: Vahl enjoyed the attention, and Sigismond was pleased at his own cleverness.

Of all those who passed by, Vahl liked best to see Artur and his father. Since the day they had come to his rescue in the forest, they never passed him without a friendly word. When Sir Olivier attended a conference of the leaders in the great hall, Artur waited for him in the courtyard. One day, tired of doing nothing, he proposed a bout of swordplay with Vahl. After that they engaged on several occasions. Artur, who gained advantage from his speed, lost it by his rashness to Vahl's steadier weapon. They were evenly matched.

One evening Father Bernard, who had been staying in a monastery outside the city, came into the castle yard. Spying Vahl on his bench, he sat down with him for a chat. At that moment Sir Olivier and Artur went by, wearing the garnet robes in which Vahl had first seen them. Vahl chuckled to himself when he saw that Artur's hands were still bare. Knight and squire waved their usual cheerful greeting.

"There go two gallant gentlemen!" exclaimed the priest.

"Gallant indeed!" Vahl agreed. "I never knew a noble knight or squire to speak so free and friendly to any churl beneath them as those two speak to me."

"That sounds like Olivier of Artois," Father Bernard nodded. "If other men were as kind as he, Satan would be a lonely soul."

"How does it happen that Sir Olivier dines so often with the kings?" Vahl asked.

The good monk looked surprised. "Why not? He is one of the greatest soldiers in the army."

"He is not one of the commanders," Vahl objected.

"He could have been, had he chosen to bring his own men," Father Bernard explained. "Surely you know he is a great lord! He was born heir to estates in Artois. Those he lost, but he fought for and won larger lands in Italy, and those he holds."

"What is a great lord doing with no followers but a young squire, making his way with minstrelsy?"

"How you could live among the Burgundians, and not know that story —" began Father Bernard, incredulously. His eyes sparkled with the prospect of a good tale to tell. "He was an eldest son, destined to rule. He could handle a sword like Saint Michael himself, and when he was a stripling squire, he disguised himself in borrowed armor, entered a tournament, and unhorsed the very knight he served after that worthy had beaten all his opponents! Then he went gaily from tournament to tournament, winning far more crowns than scars, till all the northern countries rang with his prowess. But in a bout he wounded one of his friends in the lists, so grievously that the young knight died. None other blamed Sir Olivier, but he blamed himself; he broke his lance and would not joust again. He shamed his father by taking up a harp and roaming abroad like a common minstrel. The people loved his merry lays, and his songs were sung all over Artois.

"Once as he rode homeward he heard one of his hymns trilled by what sounded like an angel's voice. It belonged to a beautiful peasant girl, and he paid court to her. His father raved and shut his son up in a tower room till he should repent of his folly. Sir Olivier jumped out of his window into the moat below that night, persuaded his father's bridge-tender to fish him out so he would not muddy his apparel on the slippery banks, and clean but damp married the maiden before dawn. His father's men caught them both at the priest's house. The old knight cast his son into the keep, but the jailer was Sir Olivier's friend and helped him escape. His wife was gone, no one knew where. He went to his

wife's family, but they would not take him in for
fear of his father. He would never have got away but
the priest who had married him gave him a horse to
ride south.

"Sir Olivier vowed that he would force his
father to right the wrong he had done. He joined
a Free Company and hired himself out with them to
an Italian prince. Soon he was leading the company
from victory to victory. In five years he had wealth
and honor and a peerless band of soldiers.

"Then he took his men to Artois and camped
at his father's gate. He declared that if his father
returned his wife to him alive he would depart, leaving his young brother to inherit. But if his wife
were dead, he would lay siege to his father's castle
and starve everyone in it. His father sent posthaste
to the convent where he had hidden the girl. She
still lived, but she was sick and weak from fasting
and prayer; she had mortified herself to gain heaven's
grace, so that God would help Sir Olivier find her.
Sir Olivier's father repented his treatment of his son,
and begged him to remain and take his rightful
place in Artois, but Sir Olivier would not. He took
his wife to Italy and built her a castle in the sunny
south. There she died giving birth to her son.

"Then Sir Olivier vowed that since he had been
so long separated from her he loved, he would never
be separated from her child. He could not bring the
babe up on a battlefield and he cared little for his

empty home. He took up his harp again and roamed from court to court, trading his music for kindness to his child. Since then he has fought only for his own lands and his Church."

"Has he not long since become more minstrel than warrior?" Vahl asked.

Sadly the priest shook his cowled head. "Think you the warfare for our faith ever ends? These are troubled times in Italy. Sir Olivier has valiantly defended the Church in Rome against many enemies. His sword has gathered no rust."

John of Nevers let no sunny day go by in Buda without indulging in his favorite sport. It was customary for him to invite on his hawking parties various French leaders from other divisions, and if they did not bring their hawks, he loaned them his — any but Crusader. On such sallies he ordered Vahl to accompany the horsemen, since an injured bird might require quick attention.

These hunts weighed Vahl down with responsibility, but also buoyed him up with pride that he rode among the captains of the crusade. Frequently Sir Olivier accompanied Count John's train. His presence always brought Vahl double pleasure, since where he went, Artur followed. Then the boys rode side by side, Artur intent on Vahl's birdlore, and Vahl covertly studying the young aristocrat's words and manner.

They heard, of course, the talk among the leaders and discussed together the future of the crusade. Vahl was astonished at the way the French knights joked about the Turkish army which they expected to meet. He supposed that the Turks who had driven the Christians out of the Holy Land must be terrible fighters, but of all the French leaders there was only one who did not make light of the Turks' prowess.

This one, iron-strong, swarthy Sir James de Helly, had served in Turkey as a soldier under the father of Bajazet, and of all the company he alone could speak the Turkish language. He described the Turks as worthy foemen, and warned the others not to underrate them. But the others treated his warnings as a huge jest.

Artur, like his father and the others, laughed at Sir James, and jeered at Vahl for believing that the knight might speak truth. Why should the French fear the Turks, since it was well known that French chivalry was superior to any other in Europe?

It had been early March in the year 1396 when Sigismond received word from Bajazet that the Sultan would lead a Turkish army across the Danube in May. It had been in late March that the French set forth to help the Hungarians. They came into Buda in April, and there made preparations for their march against the Turks: putting their armor in order, preparing great stores of provisions, and

35

holding many mimic battles to increase their skill at arms. When May came, they were ready to march eastward.

But Sigismond did not want to set his army in motion until he could learn what the movement of the Turkish army might be. No further word came from Bajazet, and the Hungarian scouts sent out to spy upon his movements returned with the news that he was still in Asia.

When the king heard this, he called a council of the crusaders to consider how they should act in the face of this disappointment. All the lords agreed that they had come together to distinguish themselves by acts of chivalry. If Bajazet would not keep his promise to meet them in Europe, they ought to continue their expedition into Turkey. God willing, they would first defeat Bajazet, then conquer Syria and the Holy Land, and deliver Jerusalem from the infidels.

King Sigismond and the marshals of the armies of France, Germany, Austria, Bohemia, and their allies issued orders therefore that everyone should be prepared to march on the octave of St. John the Baptist. Their orders were heeded; in every camp and courtyard servants worked busily preparing everything for their masters' wants.

"Truly God has raised up a great army to restore the land of the unbelievers to Holy Church," Father Bernard said to Vahl as they began to march.

"There are more than sixty thousand in this array!"
He gazed with shining eyes upon ranks of knights,
lancers, swordsmen, archers, and crossbowmen, all
faring forth to the crusade.

Vahl marveled at the number who had willingly
left their homes to fight in God's cause. There
were so many that when they reached the banks of
the Danube River, where barges, boats, and pon-
toons had been prepared for their crossing into
enemy territory, it was more than eight days before
they all passed over.

The lower Danube River divided the kingdoms
of Hungary and Turkey, but the Christians landed
in pleasant meadows, from which the inhabitants
had fled away to the nearest fortified cities. There
was no sign of an enemy army. The scouts who had
been sent ahead came back to report that they could
learn no word of Bajazet.

The divisions which crossed the river first encamped beside it to wait for their comrades. While
they waited, they celebrated their arrival in Turkey
with sport and feasting, mock battles and tourneys.
On the day that the last of the army entered Turkey,
Count John of Nevers was created a knight by King
Sigismond at a ceremony in the summer sunshine.
Vahl glowed with pride as he watched from a distant hill the king's sword striking the shoulder of
the kneeling knight.

Soon Vahl had his own part in the day's festival. The new Sir John, having had no hawking on the march from Buda, sent for his falcons and invited a few friends to spend the rest of the day in hunting with him.

Scouts had searched over many miles for a Turkish army and found none, so it was known that if any Turkish forces lurked in the neighborhood, they must be small. To avoid any danger, however, the Count of Nevers sent an advance guard of knights and squires to make a great circle in the nearby hills, ordering them to report any suspicious sight to the huntsmen. Artur was among those sent as scouts; Vahl attended Sir John.

At intervals, as the half dozen hunters rode toward the hills, one of the advance guard would return to report that the land seemed empty of people. It had not been empty long, for neat whitewashed houses dotted the plain. Beneath the thatched roofs bright strings of red peppers dried in the sun. Sheep grazed about, and an occasional stolid black buffalo. Grapes hung on trellised vines, and juicy melons lay on the ground. The knights plucked a few bunches of grapes, and ate them as they cantered on.

The other hawks had all been flown at prey before Count John saw a bird which he considered worthy of his Greenland falcon's skill. It was a kite, high on the wing, gliding as if on a strong wind. With its forked tail, it looked much like a huge swallow. Swiftly the Count unhooded his giant bird.

"Gaze, ho!" he cried, tossing her upward.

Each stroke of Crusader's strong wings sent her on a bounding leap as if she climbed invisible stairs into heaven. The kite, seeing her in pursuit, flew quickly upward in small deep circles. The falcon beat her wings faster; while the kite rose in its narrow spiral, Crusader rose with greater speed in wider rings. She gained the sky above the darting kite, so high that she was almost invisible to the watchers below. Her wings shivered and stretched out. Down she plummeted. The falcon's claws missed the kite by a feather's breadth; she fell far below before she recovered from her dive. Then up she shot once more after the still-rising kite, once more began to circle, and once more took the sky above her prey.

The hunters galloped rapidly in the direction the flight had taken, all eyes on the chase. Vahl stuck close at their heels until he came to the top of a little hillock sloping toward a marshy lake. Seeing Crusader poised to strike again, he stopped to watch. The falcon hurtled down, her path a dark streak of lightning as she struck.

In that same instant, out of the brush which covered the hillside, rose a score of turbaned bowmen on all sides of the horsemen.

Vahl shouted a wild warning, but his cry was drowned out in the hubbub. The Turk nearest the boy had not seen him but was aiming his arrow at the last knight in the train, and his bowstring was already taut. With no time to think, Vahl kicked his horse violently forward and rode the Turk down. When the man struggled to his feet, Vahl's sword was out and ready; he thrust savagely at the man's right arm before the dazed creature recovered himself. Vahl turned to take on another antagonist, but Sir John de Vienne shouted, "Go for help!" and he wheeled his horse. The nearest Turk covered him with an arrow already in his bow. Vahl ducked low on his horse's neck; the arrow whistled through his hair. He galloped back the way the hunters had come, shouting for help as he rode.

A quarter of a mile away, he heard an answering hail. Three of the armed scouts, with their three squires, galloped toward him. The boy led them at top speed back to the encounter.

The French knights, hampered as all but John were by the birds on their wrists and lacking any weapons but their swords, had still been well enough protected by their shirts of mail to put up a stiff fight. Six Turks lay stretched groaning on the ground; the others, though still two-to-one against the knights, were only peasants, unskilled in arms. When the fully armed scouts burst into the melee, it was soon over. Eight Turks lay dying; the others were trussed together and led back to camp.

"You came at the right time, for our need was

sore," John of Nevers commended the men. An arrow had grazed his thigh and a spear had pierced one calf, but he had no serious wounds and his companions had suffered little more.

The falcons were the chief casualties on the French side. A peregrine had flown away and could not be recaptured. A goshawk, cast off, had become entangled by its jesses in a nearby tree. Fortunately a squire was able to climb up and bring it down. But three, on the hunters' wrists when the attack came, had been slain. The great Greenland falcon had disappeared.

Count John's pleasure in the outcome of the battle was instantly dimmed when he realized that it had cost him his favorite bird. Wounded as he was, he insisted on riding at once with some of the knights to try to retrieve the hawk. But he was overruled and forced to ride back to camp where Father Bernard could dress his wounds.

"Think not I blame you for the loss of the bird," Count John told Vahl. "Had you been of knightly blood, you could have done no more in helping us put down our enemies."

Nevertheless Vahl mourned the great white bird which had been his master's pride. Perhaps, he thought, lying wakeful through the night, it would be worthwhile trying to recapture the hawk though it might never be seen again; it could not possibly have any feeling of attachment to the strange land in which it flew. Only his voice, or Count John's, would have any familiarity in its ears. Count John could not pursue it; that left Vahl to try.

The early summer dawn scarcely glimmered in the east before the boy was in his saddle, picking his way quietly out of camp across the river valley toward the rolling hills. He wore no shirt of mail, but his well-padded leathern jacket and hood would give him some protection against stray arrows. He had no fear that Turks lurked near any longer. Undoubtedly the previous day's encounter had frightened away the few who had remained near their homes when the main army of the Christians first crossed the river.

Outside the outposts of the Christian camp, Vahl saw neither man nor woman, though he rode near several farmyards. Fruit hung unplucked in the orchards; chickens and geese scratched untended in the fields; goats grazed quietly on the grassy meadows, but the farm people had all disappeared. Vahl stopped to milk a goat to stay his hunger. The poor creature seemed to welcome his touch, being in misery with full udders which her master had not come to relieve. Vahl patted the goat, when his thirst was satisfied, and hastened on. He knew that in an hour or two scouts would round up the peasants' livestock for milk and meat to provision the army.

He had ridden but little farther when he heard

a party of horsemen behind him. They galloped quickly toward him. The foremost one shouted, and Vahl recognized Sir Olivier's voice.

"Have you seen Artur?"

Vahl's heart sank, and he shook his head. "I looked for him in vain last night. Is he lost?"

"I had hoped he was with you," said Sir Olivier, bleakly. "No one has seen him since the hunt."

"If you go to seek him now, let me join you," Vahl begged. "I came to seek Sir John's white falcon; we can aid each other."

"If you seek a falcon that has tasted freedom, you have faith in miracles," remarked the oldest horseman in the party.

"Our Lord came to seek and to save that which was lost. He will surely bless our efforts to follow His example," Vahl said stoutly. He thought to himself that if it was folly to seek a lost falcon in these wilds, it was still more hopeless to search for a young scout who had evidently met a band of Turkish soldiers and been slain. Yet he shrank from thinking of that fate for Artur, and he was glad of what he had said when Sir Olivier's worried face relaxed, and the knight said devoutly, "Amen!"

As the sun rose higher, its heat made the very air shimmer under the blazing sky. The horsemen were drenched in sweat when they reached the battleground.

One of the Turks still moaned faintly, though

his eyes were glazed with death. A knight released him from pain with his misericorde, and murmured a Christian prayer over him. The dead Turks the knights paid scant heed to, beyond noting that they had been left untouched. Evidently no comrades had ventured near their bodies, which seemed to hint that no other armed force was in the neighborhood. The knights decided to scatter widely, searching for Artur. Vahl rode down toward the marsh where the falcon had struck the kite to earth the day before.

All day he watched sky and earth without a sign of bird or friend. His horse grazed nearby. Occasionally he heard the horsemen shouting, as they came together, consulted, and set off to search anew. At last they gathered and signaled to him that their search had been useless.

Vahl waved back, leadenhearted for both Artur and Crusader. He had his foot in his stirrup when his watchful eye saw two moving specks of white in the sky between nearby hills. The lower was a lazy-flying stork. The other . . . Scarcely daring to believe his eyes, he saw a white streak plummet down. Only Crusader had the incredible speed of that dive!

Pointing, he shrieked at the knights. They galloped toward him. He careened toward the gap between the hills, the knights some distance behind.

Vahl found himself in a shrubby glade, quite sunny, with tall trees on the hillsides all around.

He halted, watching the falcon on its circling flight until it had outsped its prey and struck it to earth.

"A quick kill, that!" one of the horsemen said approvingly, riding up to him. "But now you have found your bird, how can you catch her?"

"I know not," Vahl answered frankly. "Wait here for me; I can only try."

The bird had bound to the limp body of the stork on the ground. Vahl knew that if it would respond to a call, that moment was the time. Heart thumping, he took a breath to shout. Another shout, as like his own as his very father's had been, pierced the air. Vahl whirled angrily on the horsemen, but their faces were as startled as his own. The five gazed, worried, over the undergrowth around them, and their hands sought their swords.

Vahl, eyes glued to the bird, saw that, obedient to the call, it rose and descended into a brushy tangle. Quiet reigned over the vale for the time of a long breath. Then Sir Olivier shouted.

"Artur!"

He spurred his horse toward the brush that concealed the bird. The others, still uncertain whether they dealt with Turk or Christian, drew their swords and followed.

A faint cry answered Sir Olivier. When the knights reached its source, they found Artúr, wounded, on the ground. The falcon perched on his wrist, its jesses firmly in his hand.

"The Turks found me," the squire explained, as Vahl hooded and took the bird, and Sir Olivier knelt to examine the arrow wound in his leg. "They killed my horse under me but my hurt did not disable me completely. I dropped out of sight into the brush. They must have thought me as good as dead. I thought I was, myself, last night when I lay here parched and weak from loss of blood. But this morning I saw the falcon. I knew you would seek it, Vahl. When it came at my call, I hoped again."

"Not in vain, thank God!" cried his father passionately. "Ah, falconer!" he said to Vahl, reaching up to touch his hand, "my son and I owe much to you and your bird."

"But how did you know what call to use?" Vahl asked Artur, embarrassed at the knight's praise. "Your call was my father's call exactly. The hawk was trained to it, and I thought none but Sir John and I knew it."

The squire's eyes twinkled in his fever-flushed face. "Ever since that day in the camp," he confessed, "I have longed for the time when I could call that bird to me under your very nose. Many a day have I mocked your call, safe out of your hearing."

Vahl laughed. "You shall carry Crusader to Count John and receive his thanks," he promised. "He prizes her above all his possessions, and without you she might have been lost to him forever."

"And without you I would have been lost to the

46

whole world forever," said Artur. "What say you —
let us go to him together? Hereafter perhaps he
will let me fly the hawk with you. Then, Father,
you will owe me your gloves!"

"Whatever Sir John does, you have earned them
and they are yours," said Sir Olivier.

He finished binding up the boy's wound with
what skill he could, using strips of cloth torn from
his tunic. Then Sir Olivier carried his son back to
camp, holding Artur in the saddle as he rode behind.

Freed of fear, Artur showed quick strength.
When Father Bernard had dressed his wound and he
had broken his fast, Artur proudly took the falcon
on his fist, and limped beside Vahl into the presence
of John of Nevers.

In his delight the Count flung them his purse,
well filled with silver coins, laughed over the story
of the wager and the gloves, and called on Sir Olivier
to celebrate the bird's return in worthy verse.

Each day afterward, while the army stayed in
camp, John rode hunting with Crusader on his fist,
Artur and Vahl riding on his right and left hand
carrying other hawks. But that was only for a short
time. Leaders of the crusade, having rested their
weary troops, determined to advance against the
cities of the Turks.

3

Battle

HE KING OF HUNGARY and his allies decided to besiege the town of Comecte, to which the people of that region had fled. The lords resented the base attack which had been made on Sir John's little pleasure party. They meant to teach the infidels that they behaved unchivalrously at their peril.

The town was built on an open plain beside the Mecte River, which rose in Turkey and fell into the Danube near the sea. About the town clustered many little farms with their orchards and vineyards. The Turks were forbidden by their religion to taste wine, but they bottled it in goatskins, and had profited for generations from their wine trade with the Christians. The contents of many full skins, and fresh grapes, found in the country, rejoiced the besiegers while they prepared their attacks.

At first the townsfolk opposed them valiantly, but they were soon overwhelmed by hunger and the great numbers of the crusaders. The city was taken by storm. The defenders were put to the sword.

Not being a man-at-arms, Vahl took no part in the attack. But he heard the din of the battle and saw the flame and smoke of the burning houses rise until even the spires of the minarets were blotted from sight.

From Comecte the army advanced farther into Turkey to a town called Laquaire. This was not taken and destroyed until it had been besieged fifteen days, so stout was its defense.

The next town, Brehappe, was even stronger. The Turkish knight in command was an experienced soldier and he had a strong garrison. The Christians burned the town, which lay outside the castle stronghold, but did not stay to take the fort. As the summer was passing, they thought it best to conquer the greater city of Nicopolis, on the Danube, which was more worthy of their strength. Sigismond of Hungary led his troops onward, and the whole army encamped around Nicopolis and laid siege to it.

But there were some lords among the besiegers who preferred quick action to slow siege. Among these was the French Lord de Coucy. He called for volunteers to accompany him on a foray deeper into Turkey. He selected Hungarian guides, who promised to find enemy troops for them to fight if the enemy had any army in the country. Eight hundred mounted crossbowmen, lancers, and knights, among them Sir Olivier and Artur, joined the expedition. Vahl longed to go too, to help fight men of their own mettle; but he dared not leave his birds, both of which seemed to be weakening in the great heat.

No word came back of the Lord de Coucy's party for five days. At sunset on the sixth the horsemen appeared against the golden sky, cantering back in triumph with a cheerful tale to tell. They had met and vanquished an army of twenty thousand Turks, with scarcely any losses of their own.

"It was a great feat!" Artur boasted gaily to Vahl. "We rode for two days without seeing any Turks except a few scared peasants. But on the third day the Hungarian scouts told us that a great army of Turks was waiting for us in ambush on the other side of a wood.

"Lord de Coucy said, 'We must advance and see what kind of people they are; for since we have come this far, we must not return without offering them combat.' All the other lords agreed. But they halted at the wood and posted all of us there except a hundred, who rode forward as if they were the whole troop. When the Turks saw them, they came out of their ambush and advanced. Our men fled, with the Turks in pursuit. The rest of us stayed hidden in the woods until both our advance troop and the infidels had passed through. Then we attacked the Turks from behind, while our comrades wheeled and attacked them in front. We threw their whole army into such confusion that thousands of them tried to flee away without fighting. We slew them in heaps."

"Now, I think, we will see some action," Sir Olivier added. "If Bajazet does not lead his army against us to avenge this defeat, he is no true warrior."

But there was no sign of Bajazet's army, though Hungarian scouts went out to watch for it every day. The Christian host lay about Nicopolis inactive. Only a few restless horsemen occasionally made a sally against some weak point in the city's defenses to relieve the monotony of waiting for the defenders to be starved out.

Autumn was coming on. As it was plain that Nicopolis could not hold out much longer without help from Bajazet, the Christians already regarded it as theirs.

The King of Hungary called a council of the French lords, and proposed to them that, as soon as Nicopolis fell, they should return with him to the castles and halls he had prepared for them. There they could spend the winter pleasantly while stores for another summer campaign were prepared.

"We will get large reinforcements," said Sigismond, "and then next summer, if it please God, we will cross the Hellespont and conquer the Holy Land. Surely, after he has heard of our great deeds of arms this season, Bajazet will not refuse to meet us. Then we can fight and destroy him."

The French lords approved this program, and continued to take their ease outside Nicopolis, waiting for the besieged Turks to sally forth and be killed, or to surrender from starvation.

Sir John of Nevers, meanwhile, had been suffering from a slight fever which forced him to forego the Lord de Coucy's sally. Though he recovered enough in a few days to leave his bed, and longed to hunt, he had not strength to sit in his saddle. While he grew stronger, therefore, his hawks were left to Vahl to fly. Occasionally, as a mark of favor, he bade one of his knights use the darker falcon; but Vahl alone flew Crusader.

On the Monday before Michaelmas day, Vahl took the two falcons out for prey. He would have liked Artur's company, but the squire was busy polishing Sir Olivier's plate armor, and Vahl rode through camp looking for a companion.

Near the last outpost, Sir James de Helly hailed him.

"What price the loan of a bird, young falconer? My own is dead of the heat, and I am hungry for a bit of sport."

Vahl welcomed his company gladly, and the

big goshawk was soon mounted on Sir James's fist. Vahl knew that whatever the knights thought of Sir James's ideas about the Turks, they acknowledged him a skillful falconer. Any bird would be safe in his hands.

Scouts for the army continually roamed over all the nearby territory, watching for a possible Turkish force. Vahl and Sir James therefore exercised no caution, but wandered freely away from the camp. Farther and farther they rode, looking for better game than was left near the town.

At last Sir James's bird took a rabbit. Shortly afterward, Vahl flew Crusader at a stork, and the hunters galloped forward, following the flight toward the kill. They watched hawk and prey fall beyond a rise of ground. Suddenly, rounding the hill, they saw far off a great body of horsemen.

"The Turks!" cried Sir James de Helly, after an instant of startled silence. "Quick! Into this clump of willows!"

Hidden, they stared out through the leaves. "The infidels have defiled through the mountain passes from the south while we watched for them in the east!" muttered Sir James.

"How can you be so sure they are enemies?" Vahl asked, peering intently.

"Look! It is the army of Bajazet himself! See that huge pennant with the blood-red star and crescent towering above the others. It bears a crown also, which none but he may do! Come — we must warn the camp!"

"Go, go!" Vahl begged him. "The bird has come down so close, I cannot bear to leave her. I can get her safely and follow you. They have not seen us."

"We endanger the whole camp if we both stay," said Sir James, gnawing his mustache. "I must go! God help you!"

He set spurs to his horse, dodged quickly to the protection of a slight bluff by the nearby stream, and was safely out of sight. Vahl jumped down, left his horse hidden in the willows and crawled from clump to clump of underbrush toward the falcon and its prey. He could see the horsemen riding nearer and nearer, an endless company. They gave no sign that they had seen him.

All might have gone well, but as he neared Crusader and softly called, he had to crouch behind a bush to remain hidden. The bird, unable to see him but answering the call, took wing and fluttered briefly in the air. Distant though they were, Vahl could hear some of the horsemen shout at the sight. Only speed could save him. He leaped forward, hooded the bird with fumbling hands, and ran.

He knew the horsemen could not fail to see him, but they were still some distance away. He had but a short space to cover before he reached the comparative safety of the willows, and he trusted in his nimble legs. But an old limb, buried in the grass, sent him sprawling. Before he could scramble up, he saw that two horsemen had left the main body of troops to give him chase, and already had covered half the distance between them. In panic he ran faster than he had ever run before. He reached his horse in the willow thicket and kicked the beast to furious speed.

With relief he saw that he was outdistancing his pursuers. He laughed aloud; once over the crest of the next hill, he would be safe among trees. He would have a great tale to tell Artur about his escape.

But the Turks would not let him get away so easily. An arrow whistled past his ears. Outlined against the sky as he rode over the hill, he made a perfect target. The Turks were skilled marksmen, and the second arrow struck his horse in its hind-quarters. The animal slackened pace but kept limping on until a third arrow embedded itself in his leg and brought him to the earth.

Vahl leaped from his saddle and panted toward the summit of the hill. He had almost gained the shelter of the woods when an arrow pierced his thick leathern tunic and entered his shoulder. The force of the blow sent him spinning.

The Turks rode up beside him. With an *Ave* on his lips, the terrified boy closed his eyes and waited for them to strike him dead. His wound made his

sword arm useless, and the bird still perched unharmed on his left wrist.

Vahl heard the Turks talking back and forth.
Still muttering a prayer under his breath, he ventured to look for them and found them staring
at the falcon. Neither offered to do him any harm.
One took the bird on his own fist; the other took a
rope which dangled from his saddle, bound the boy's
hands together, and led him like a tethered colt
toward the main troop.

Having rejoined their companions, the two
Turks exchanged short words with a heavily bearded
knight Vahl realized must be their commander. Then
they lifted their hands in salute and continued to
lead Vahl on in the direction from which they had
advanced. Their course took them far to one side,
for the Turkish vanguard was shaped like a spear-
head, narrow in front and spreading out behind.
Vahl realized that no mere company was advancing
here against the Christians. It was an army, in set
formation, stern and disciplined. He saw with sinking heart that the knights in it compared well with
the Christians in bearing, equipment, and weapons.
They differed most in the darkness of their features
and in the white turbans which they wore instead of
helmets above their swirling cloaks.

There seemed no end to their marching column.
When the van had all gone by, a second cloud of dust
rising over the plain resolved itself into another

multitude of Turkish horsemen. Vahl's captors withdrew still farther to the side, but kept on their way past the advancing horde.

Vahl's wound began to throb painfully. Fever rose in his blood. It seemed to his tired eyes that the whole world was full of rushing Turkish troops. Their numbers he could not judge: they seemed countless. He murmured a prayer of gratitude that Sir James de Helly had escaped to warn the Christian host of their approach. In their swift march the Turks must have taken the Hungarian scouts by surprise and were hoping to come unheralded upon the main body of their enemy.

At last Vahl and his captors emerged from the clouds of choking dust raised by the horsemen. Before them stretched a huge Turkish camp on the grassy plain. Men darted busily everywhere. More troops were forming on one side. The two Turkish horsemen threaded their way between the tents to the very center of the camp. There they dismounted, tossed their horses' bridles to a turbanned guard, and jerked Vahl inside a gigantic pavilion.

In the sudden change from the dazzling light outside, Vahl could scarcely make out his surroundings; he staggered blindly. The men pushed him to a bench and sat waiting silently. The heat was stifling. As Vahl's eyes adjusted themselves to the shadowed interior, he saw that he was in an antechamber as large as an ordinary tent. Just then the

Turkish rugs which formed the inner wall were parted; a bronzed face emerged and a soft message was spoken. Instantly his captors pulled Vahl to his feet and into the body of the tent.

The pavilion was furnished with sumptuous elegance. Priceless carpets made its walls and floor. Its divans were covered by magnificent embroideries. Its tables were set with silver ewers and basins; one bore luscious fruit on a platter of gold.

In the center of all this magnificence stood a tall man, black-bearded and swarthy, with burning black eyes. Of his form Vahl could make out little, for he had on a coat of mail and was being helped into his surcoat and a loose mantle by two attendants. But seeing that the two Turks fell to their knees in his presence, and pushed Vahl to his, he guessed that they knelt to the Emperor Bajazet, whom the French knights had come so far to meet.

The emperor turned frowning toward their intrusion, and addressed his men in a harsh voice that crackled with fury. Suddenly he paused; he had noticed the white falcon, still on the soldier's wrist. His tone changed. Excited phrases poured from his lips, answered by the humble tones of his followers. He lifted the falcon to his own fist and stroked it delicately, murmuring to it softly, staring, meanwhile, at the boy crouched at his feet. Abruptly, with a gesture that swept everything around him from his mind, he placed Crusader on Vahl's wrist, motioned

58

to him to rise, and pointed to his captors as if to say, "Go with them." Then he turned his back, while his squires buckled on his great curved sword.

The Turks rose from their knees and beckoned Vahl to follow them. Through the camp they strode, to a cluster of tents set apart on the river bank. They raised a shout; a dozen men came running, several carrying hawks. Gesticulating, they must have given the emperor's commands to the chief of their audience, for the man they singled out bowed low. At that they lifted their hands in salute and went away.

The Turks with whom he had been left stood and looked at Vahl, even feeling his blond hair, and plainly discussing him among themselves. At last they seemed to come to some agreement. The leader pointed; a man without a hawk stepped forward and signed to Vahl to follow him.

"Yusuf," he said smiling, pointing to himself.

Vahl's fearful heart throbbed with relief. Perhaps his life was not over after all. The man's brown face seemed friendly.

"Vahl," he answered, pointing at himself.

The man nodded, and pointed to Crusader. "Falco?" he queried, using the Latin word.

Vahl nodded. "Falco groenlandicus," he agreed.

Yusuf clapped his hands and beamed. With several of his fellows tagging behind, he led the way between the nearest tents.

Vahl knew where he was — in the encampment of Bajazet's falconers. He remembered once hearing Sir James de Helly say that the emperor kept seven hundred men to care for his hawks. Not more than a score surrounded Vahl, but Bajazet's passion for the sport of kings was clear enough. One large tent was fitted as a mews. Outside, unhooded birds basked on their perches in the sunshine. Vahl counted about three dozen, many of them magnificent, and four first cousins to the falcon he carried. They were falcons from Iceland or Norway. Not quite as large or fierce as Crusader, and darker in color, they still drew Vahl's admiration. He tried to tell the men so. He could not guess how much of his meaning they understood, but they seemed to realize that he recognized the finest birds, and they respected his judgment.

An empty block was set near the others, and the men motioned to him to leash Crusader on it. Then they sat on the grass trying to make conversation by signs. Vahl did his best to answer, but he grew weak and dizzy from the heat and the fever from his wound. Darkness seemed to rise up and cover him.

When he opened his eyes again he lay in one of the tents. The leather of his jacket had been cut away from his shoulder, and the wound dressed with strong-smelling ointment and roughly bandaged. Yusuf had roused him, handing the boy a goatskin bottle of milk. Vahl drank the milk gratefully, and would have sunk to sleep had not the man shaken him and motioned that he should rise. Painfully Vahl did so, and followed Yusuf outside.

The camp was being broken up. Men were everywhere, working, shouting, singing, dancing, as if they were riotous with drink. Vahl knew that the religion of the Mohammedans forbade them to take intoxicating liquors; their excitement must be due to some other cause. Only half-conscious as he still was, it took all his energy to follow the commands of his guide. Yusuf led him toward a horse and bound his painful right arm to the stirrup by a short rope. Then he handed him Crusader to carry, mounted, and joined a motley cavalcade of soldiers and camp followers setting out across the plain.

Vahl's head cleared as they went. The pace was slow, the milk had strengthened him, and the ointment on his shoulder eased its pain. The heat was even more intense than before; the sun's rays burned from the afternoon sky. Vahl squinted against the glare, paying little attention to the line of march. Then suddenly he recognized familiar ground. They were retracing the path over which he had been brought that morning. His mind came alive with horrified speculation. The Turks had gone to do battle with the Christians. Now that they were moving forward their main army, did it mean that they hoped for victory? Or had they already won?

Above the clatter and talk of the riders among whom he walked, Vahl began to hear shouts and songs, faint and far away. Then came the metallic din of steel striking steel, punctuated by screams. The battle was not over.

The distant noises grew and grew. As the camp train moved around the last low hill which separated it from the side meadows around Nicopolis, the furor became deafening. Dust veiled the field, and Vahl and his companions were separated from the strife by long lines of waiting, silent Turkish soldiers. It was impossible to guess the progress of the battle.

Several officers detached themselves from their troops and shouted orders. The camp train broke apart into organized groups. Yusuf and his companions retired with their gear to the bank of a small stream. Busily they worked at setting up their tents, the mews, the blocks. Vahl, released from the stirrup, was motioned to care for his own bird.

Paying no more attention to the clamor of the battle than they would have paid to the twittering of a wild bird, the falconers fed and petted their charges. Having done so, they squatted down near them over a burning charcoal brazier and began to cook food for themselves.

Vahl squatted beside them, but he chose the side of the fire facing the battle. Fearfully he watched for some sign of the outcome.

4

Disaster

AHL HAD NOT LONG to wait. Parties of Turks, herding Christian prisoners before them, began to ride through the reserve lines of their army. Pandemonium broke out. At sight of each new group of bedraggled and wounded Christians, whether Hungarians, Germans, or French, the Turks shouted with wild delight. The Christians were paraded among the tents, with the infidels jeering and spitting upon them. Vahl sickened at the sight.

He grew pale, and one of the men nearby clapped him cruelly upon his wounded shoulder, shouting some mockery. Yusuf, however, struck the man's hand aside, sputtering a protest in which Vahl caught the single word "Bajazet." He was jeered at no more. Bajazet's own command must have spared him to care for the Greenland falcon.

Dusk began to fall, but the troops of prisoners brought into the camp grew larger and larger. The clash of arms diminished, though the screaming of wounded men grew shriller and harsher as the hours wore on. Vahl caught sight of several standards he knew, borne in triumph by Moslem horsemen. Flaunted in the Turkish camp, the pennons could only mean that their owners were dead or prisoners.

Vahl sat on the warm, dry ground and bowed his aching head in his arms, trying in vain to close his ears as well as his eyes to the evidences of defeat. But his curiosity was stronger than his fear. He wrenched his eyes open in time to see Count John of Nevers and five of his leading knights, in heavy chains like common criminals. They moved under guard, and their rich raiment was torn and soiled with dust and blood, but their heads were still high. They bore themselves, even in adversity, with pride and courage. Groaning, Vahl covered his face with his hands.

The Turks spread out their army around the city; the twinkling campfires marked their places as the stars began to appear. Out from Nicopolis came the besieged citizens to join in the rejoicing. The Moslem army fed them from what seemed an inexhaustible store. Having gorged themselves, the Turks wandered around the camp, jeering at the Christians who had starved them, offering their enemies tempting morsels of food, then snatching

64

them away. The prisoners, so far as Vahl could see from a small group or two near him, were given neither food nor water.

Amid all the procession of prisoners, Vahl watched anxiously for Artur, for Sir Olivier, and for Father Bernard, but no one of them came in sight. Sir James de Helly was led by, but too distant for speech.

As the influx of captives stopped, Vahl saw that Turkish officers began to go around from group to group. Bajazet himself passed, roaring with laughter, watching the spectacle. He was followed by a long Moslem retinue, but the man with him — who was he? Unaccountably he looked familiar and made Vahl think of Paris, yet surely Vahl must be imagining some resemblance! How could a Christian be as this man was, richly dressed like a Christian lord, but neither wounded, chained, nor even sad, rather laughing loud and long with the emperor?

Suddenly Bajazet caught sight of the falcons. With a quick exclamation to his companion, he led the way toward them. The falconers instantly fell to their knees and salaamed to the ground, their faces hidden. Vahl clumsily followed their example.

The foot of one of Bajazet's attendants prodded him up. The Sultan motioned to the boy to unleash Crusader and hand him the bird. Nervously Vahl did so, and standing so close to the Sultan's companion, he suddenly knew him. He was the dark Italian

65

who had tried to take Crusader on the day the march east began! Here he stood high in favor, for Bajazet set the hawk momentarily on his outstretched fist. He raised his arm proudly with its treasured burden, poured out a torrent of words that sounded to Vahl like admiration, and returned the bird to the Sultan. In doing so he met Vahl's eyes. The smile died from his own as he stared at the boy. He, too, had remembered Paris!

He spat out a few venomous words, pointing to the boy. Bajazet looked from one to the other, laughed, and murmured a careless phrase as he handed Crusader to Vahl and turned to go. The Italian's look changed to triumph.

"A last farewell, varlet!" he sneered in French, and followed Bajazet away, leaving Vahl filled with fear. No more attention was paid to him, however; he sat down unharmed among the falconers.

Under the Sultan's eyes, those Christian knights in rich clothing were set apart, loaded with chains, and finally led away. Then, yawning, Bajazet and the Italian also departed.

The captive men-at-arms, in their leather and wool, sat hopelessly on the ground, surrounded by taunting enemies, until several Turkish officers returned from escorting the prisoner knights. At a sharp command, the disarmed Christians were prodded to their feet with blows of fist and sword. One Turk spied Vahl and advanced on him, but

Yusuf shouted him off, and the young falconer was left untouched.

The other captives were marched away like the knights, but not out of sight. The brilliant moonlight lit their shadowy shapes as they stood on the creek bank. Vahl's horrified eyes saw them thrust to their knees; he saw the flash of swords. A chorus of bloodcurdling shrieks split the air as the massacred men sprawled forward, some flat on the ground, many toppling over the bank into the creek.

Their screams were echoed and re-echoed as other groups of prisoners were slaughtered. Vahl began to shudder uncontrollably. After each outcry died, the Turks shouted and sang the more. Yet they were tired, and at last they slept. Yusuf sent Vahl into his tent, bound the boy securely to one of the wicker poles, and motioned to him to stretch out on the earth.

He lay there staring wide-eyed into the darkness. Escape? There was no hope. His life had been spared, yes; but he did not know for how long. He did not know whether to be glad or sorry that he had lived out the day. He listened to Yusuf's comfortable snores and began to tell his beads on the leather thong about his neck. Perhaps God had not forsaken him.

Yusuf roused himself in the first gray light of dawn, and stirred the boy upright with a cheerful kick. All the camp slept soundly but for three other falconers: Mehmet, Ali, and Ibrahim. Hastily the five gulped down goats' milk which Yusuf passed around in a great leathern skin. Then each of the Turks took an Iceland falcon on his wrist and mounted his horse. Contrary to the European custom, they carried the birds on their right hands. They found a horse for Vahl, also — a small and sorry beast — which they roped securely between Yusuf's and Memet's. Then they mounted him with Crusader on his fist, made a circuit of the camp, and struck off toward the northwest.

Vahl wondered whether they passed through the field of battle because they themselves were curious about the sight, or whether they did it to impress him with the mighty power of the Moslems. He could tell from their gestures and voices that they delighted in what they saw and in its effect upon him.

Vahl was stunned by the Christian tragedy. He could hardly realize what had happened. Bajazet's banner flew over the silk pavilion which had belonged to Sigismond of Hungary. The whole Christian camp had been taken over by the Turks. Beyond was the battlefield, strewn with corpses. They lay, some singly, some in heaps, by the tens and hundreds. Great hordes of flies buzzed about them, and vultures wheeled in the sky, attracted by the smell of blood. Saddest sight to Vahl was the white banner of the Virgin Mary lying in the dust, its standard still clutched in the valiant hands of Sir John de Vienne, who had died in the forefront of the fight. It was gripped, too, by Father Bernard, whose devout arms must have tried to hold it up when Sir John fell. Knight and priest lay stained and stiff, their faces in the pagan earth which they had vainly tried to claim for Christ.

The huntsmen stopped occasionally. Once they rolled over a knight dressed in silk who had a purse at his belt. His golden coins made them shout with glee. Once Ibrahim dismounted to stab to death a knight who lay groaning from his wounds. But they did not stop long. Having crossed the field, they turned their horses toward a wooded hill.

Occasionally they saw a bird wheeling above them, but at these the Turks gestured as much as to say, "I must have a better bird than that to test my hawk."

At length they saw a winging heron which seemed to please them; Yusuf gave a command, and Ali and Ibrahim unhooded and flew their cast of falcons. To fly both falcon and tiercel at a heron was a common custom; but after they had brought down their prey, and Yusuf and Mehmet likewise flew their cast at a heron, it occurred to Vahl that he might be hawking for his life. If Crusader did not do alone what the others had done in pairs — if she did not outspeed and outkill them, Vahl had no doubt that he would be put to the sword as quickly as any of the luckless bowmen the night before.

If God meant to shelter him under a bird's wing, Crusader was the bird He would have chosen out of all the world. Vahl did not fear the test, but he tried to postpone it, shaking his head scornfully and measuring out the wingspread of the bird he wanted to take, whenever a possible victim crossed the sky. Never again, Vahl knew, would he have such a chance to escape, even if he were still alive when the Sultan's army began its march back to Asia. Four armed men to one wounded and unarmed, still the odds were better for him than they might ever be again. His wits worked furiously.

The hunt turned north and west. Obviously the Turks had been assured that they need fear no lurking enemies. Yet suddenly scar-cheeked Ibrahim, the foremost, stopped, pointing. Between distant trees he had caught a flash of color.

The party galloped forward to see what it was: two Christian fugitives. Laughing, Ibrahim and Ali handed their birds to Vahl's guards, drew their swords, and rode forward.

The two knights, on foot and wounded, backed themselves against a stout tree for defense. They were clever swordsmen, but the advantage was with their mounted foes. Even so, they gave more wounds than they received before Yusuf and Mehmet rode up with Vahl between them. Vahl shouted encouragement to the knights, but Yusuf laid his hand on his sword-hilt threateningly and silenced him.

Against two assailants the weary knights might still have prevailed, but suddenly Mehmet slipped off his horse, fastened the two falcons he carried to a low branch, and sped behind the Christians, sword in hand. Too horrified to remember his own danger, Vahl cried a warning. Even if the knights heard him, they could do no more to protect themselves.

At that moment Vahl saw his own chance. While Yusuf eyed with keen enjoyment the stealthy approach of Mehmet behind the knights, Vahl furtively untied the simple knot by which Mehmet's horse was bound to his own. He vaulted from his saddle, and onto Mehmet's horse. Yusuf reached out to seize him, but too late.

Beating the horse with its bridle, Vahl rode headlong among the trees. The noise of pursuit rose behind him, but Yusuf was hampered by the slow horse fastened to his own. Ali and the others would not realize for a moment what had happened, being busy with their own battle. But soon, Vahl knew, they would be on his trail. Unarmed, he could not fight them. He might outwit them.

Scraping through a thicket of tangled shrubs, he came to a low-branched tree. With a bound he was off the horse, and had given it a blow which sent it galloping on at renewed speed. He meant to climb the tree but had no time; crouching in the briars,

71

he saw Yusuf crash by. Then there was silence. At last, moving Crusader up a limb or two at a time before him, he managed to clamber up among the leafy branches. It was agony to use his wounded arm, but agony was preferable to death.

Perhaps an hour later Yusuf passed again, leading Mehmet's recaptured horse. Vahl had a clear view of his dark face, now frowning and cruel.

After a long time a doe slipped quietly into sight, browsing on the low branches in the thicket. She gave Vahl courage, and he started down. Suddenly she sniffed the air, then bounded off. Vahl thought at first that it was his scent which had reached her, but he waited to see. Another crackling of twigs made him shrink once more against the tree trunk.

Three Turkish horsemen he had never seen before passed almost under him, going back the way he had come. One carried a rich Christian's robe and mantle slung over his knees. Behind the last, his hands bound, his face streaked with blood, walked Paul, the young Burgundian squire who had started out beside Vahl on the march from Paris. Vahl could hardly restrain himself from attempting a rescue, but he had no weapon, and the odds were certain death. Silently he watched the little procession move out of sight through the woods.

All day he waited, cramped in his leafy perch. Not until the sun began to hang low in the west did he venture down.

He had made up his mind what to do. Weaponless, he could never win safely back to France again. A sword, a bow, and a quiver full of arrows — these were the price of his life. They were to be had back upon the battlefield, if he had the courage and the luck to get them. He started back.

Then it occurred to him that perhaps the falconers had not taken the arms of the two French knights when they slew them. They lay on his backward path — if he could find a path through the pathless wood. They were worth searching for.

He found them rather easily, not very far away at the edge of the wood. He did not venture close, since it was still quite light. When he thought he would be invisible in the dusk, he slipped quietly through the trees, set the falcon on a nearby branch, and knelt beside the dead men.

The knights had sold their lives dearly. Mehmet lay beside them, his chubby, cheerful face twisted into a grin of agony. Swiftly Vahl rolled the Turk over and unfastened the great cloak he wore. He put on Mehmet's loose robe over his own leathern garb, girded himself with Mehmet's sword belt, picked up the Turk's fallen sword and thrust it in the scabbard, pulled the falconer's turban tight and clasped the cloak buckle on his shoulder.

Clad in this disguise, he set forth with beating heart toward the battlefield, the falcon once more on his fist.

Moonlight made his way clear. He came out upon the great plain near a little farm, quiet and still in the night. Hunger, almost forgotten in the excitement of the day, rose in him at sight of the small garden. There was little left in it, for the Christians had helped themselves from every farm they could reach; but he found a green melon, whose juicy pulp refreshed him. A chicken, hidden in a bush and disturbed by Vahl's approach, squawked and fluttered out. Vahl caught it with a quick pounce and wrung its neck — heaven-sent food for Crusader!

He was about to feed the bird then and there, when a horse whinnied from the other side of the little hut. The house, then, was no longer deserted! Vahl's heart stood still; he thrust the dead chicken inside his robe. Then with every bit of energy he possessed, he ran toward the building, drawing his sword. A mounted enemy could overtake him in an instant, but if he had the horse he might get away. He knew he had not been seen, for the hut was windowless.

But a tall Turk stood at the cottage door, sword in hand, as Vahl rounded the wall. The man shouted, thinking a comrade was being pursued. Vahl gestured wildly behind him, yelling. The Turk turned toward the imaginary enemy, only to have his sword struck from his hand as the squire rushed by. Before the man could recover his weapon, Vahl

had mounted the horse and slashed the beast free
of its tether by one blow of his sword. He left the
Turk panting madly in his wake, and rode up the
plain, skirting the low hills along the edge.

At dawn he hid in the woods, resting while the
horse grazed. He noticed that the saddle bags bulged.
A vision of food sent him scurrying to investigate
them. They were filled with small bits of loot — a
jeweled dagger, a velvet hood with a silver buckle,
a silver belt bearing a pouch full of coins. Doubtless
these had been of value to their owners once, but
they did not rejoice Vahl's heart half so much as
the flint and steel he found.

Feeling about in the bottom of one of the bags
to be sure he had missed nothing, Vahl's fingers
touched something soft, and drew it forth. It was
a glove, stained and dusty. He was about to throw
it away when he recognized the color and design. It
was garnet velvet, embroidered with a golden lyre
and crown.

Frantically Vahl searched through the loot once
more, but nothing else hinted of Artur. The glove
was certainly his; he had worn it proudly a dozen
times since winning it. Now where was he? Sick-
ness clutched at Vahl's stomach. Could he have deserted a friend who was an unseen, unheard prisoner
in the farm hut? Unlikely: the Turks had little use
for prisoners. There was blood on the glove. Was
the blood Artur's?

Vahl's eyes smarted as he thought of the friends he had seen slaughtered and pictured Artur among them. Still hungry and weary, he set forth again.

Though he tried to keep hidden, he came out unexpectedly at a tiny village in a little clearing. Before he could conceal himself, two men called to him. He rode forward boldly, lifting his hand in salute as he had seen some of the Turks do. As he came up to the peasants he pointed at his throat, and began to mutter gibberish plentifully interspersed with the name of Bajazet. He tried to give the impression that he had lost his way, but was carrying the falcon to the emperor. The wide-eyed villagers seemed to make something of his talk, for they pointed him back the way he had come. He pretended great gratitude and rode off in that direction until he was out of sight; then he made a wide circuit and hurried west again. When he crossed a path he avoided it; the wilder the land, the safer he felt. It was not impossible that Turkish riders had followed fleeing Christians for many miles, and it would be dangerous to risk meeting them. Carrying Crusader, he would be no more safe among Moslems or Christians than a child flaunting a bag of gold before thieves.

He took refuge in the hills. In the wilderness the hunting was better than on the plains, and Crusader must be flown and fed. Prey for Crusader meant food for Vahl also.

5

Twelve Greenland Falcons

I T WAS LATE September when Vahl escaped from the country of the infidels. In mid-December he reached France. Fever burned in his blood from his infected shoulder wound, so that he did not notice the chill of the damp air. Crusader still perched on his emaciated wrist. The Turk's horse still bore him up. The interval between his escape and his arrival he remembered, but he wondered if his memories were those of delirium, so much had he suffered.

He rode down from the low hills rimming the Paris valley on the afternoon of the third day before Christ's Mass. The winter sun, low in the west, lit the whole sky with tongues of golden flame. Their reflection burned in the winding waters of the Seine; they blazed over the multitude of roofs until they seemed to paint a Heavenly City, shining in glory to welcome a weary pilgrim home. Vahl's heart lifted with the spires of the great churches which towered above the town.

It was dusk when he reached the Porte Saint Jacques. He passed through the gate unchallenged, and made what speed he could up the rue Saint Jacques. His homesick eyes dwelt lovingly on the very stones and bricks and timbers of the houses crowding each other along the narrow street. He crossed the Petit Pont to the Île de la Cité, rode left toward the Palais de Justice, and traversed the Grand Pont from the island to the Right Bank. The towers of Notre-Dame and Sainte Chapelle, the turrets of the Palais seemed like dark candles burning on the Île to the glory of God. Even across the river to the left, the setting sun had lighted the gloomy stone battlements of the Louvre with its last rays.

The rue Saint Denis was growing dark, but even if it had been pitch black, Vahl would not have delayed. He knew every foot of its rough pavement, and such a longing welled up in him to see familiar faces and to hear friendly voices again that he forced his tired horse into a gallop which the worn creature could hardly sustain. Passers-by stared at the tattered youth with the gaunt steed and the huge white falcon as he sped by, turned into the rue Pavée-Saint-Sauveur, and pounded wildly on the great north gate of the Hôtel d'Artois.

Old Giles, the gatekeeper, his bald pate protected by a voluminous hood, peered out of his wicket. He looked twice before he believed what he saw.

"Vahl Thorfinnsson!" he ejaculated, and hastened to throw wide the gate. "How came you here?"

"I bring news to the Duke. Stable my horse, Giles," Vahl bade, vaulting to the ground and throwing him the reins. "Is Pierre in the mews?"

"Nay, he is in the great hall with the rest of the household. But stay — tell me —"

"I cannot now; I must care for this bird first," Vahl said, moving on stiff legs toward his old home. With sudden homesickness he looked across the courtyard at the weatherbeaten square wooden tower. Some pigeons were flying, as always, in and out of their cote at the top. They had not yet come to rest for the night. Crusader should feast on one tomorrow!

What joy it would have been, Vahl thought, to run up the steep wooden stairs to the little room above the mews, as he had so often done before, and burst in on Thorfinn! What joy to hear his father greet him in Norwegian, the language he always insisted on speaking in private lest his son forget his mother-tongue! But Pierre had the falconer's quarters now.

The mews, at least, seemed like home. The wooden slats at the window had already been closed to shut out the light and cut off drafts. Vahl opened them. The unhooded birds on their perches blinked at him. Mews' Pride, Duke Philip's Greenland tiercel, bated slightly at sight of Crusader. Vahl was glad to see that the birds looked healthy. And Pierre had actually remembered Thorfinn's teaching to keep the mews clean! There was no accumulation of castings, or shreds of tirings. The stone floor had been recently swept and covered with clean straw. The broom of rushes stood in its corner. The workbench held a pile of leather, and the shelves above a good supply of gear — hoods, jesses, leashes, creances, and swivels. As always, the empty blocks stood against the wall. Vahl lifted the best and set it among the other hawks. Quickly he leashed Crusader and slipped her hood. He must not dally; the whole court should hear his news before they left their meal. He closed the slats and shut the door of the darkened mews behind him. Then he ran toward the palace.

At the great hall, the doorkeeper, a husky newcomer, wrinkled his nose in disgust at sight of Vahl.

"Out, scarecrow! This is no place for beggars!"

He would have barred Vahl's way. Vahl raised his voice.

"I come with word from John of Nevers!"

The hall fell silent as if struck dumb; then a buzz of voices broke out. Men and women craned their necks to see who had spoken. Flushed with wine, Philip of Burgundy cried impatiently from his dais:

"Who spoke of John of Nevers? Bring him here!"

Vahl strode swiftly to kneel at the Duke's feet. "My lord," he begged, "forgive my bad news. Though Count John did deeds of great bravery against the Turks, he is a prisoner of Bajazet. The whole Christian army was captured or slain in battle at Nicopolis."

"What!" roared the Duke, over the gasp which swept the room. "What?" he roared again, rising, his face purpling with rage. "How know you this?"

"With my own sorry sight," Vahl answered.

"Over your shoulder, running as fast as you could, I swear!" bellowed the Duke. "Coward! Deserter! You shall eat your lying tale! Seize him, Jules and Martin! Give him twenty lashes, and cast him into the Châtelet!"

Unheeding his desperate shouts of protest, the two burly men-at-arms dragged him out of the hall.

Three days later, face downward on the cold stone floor of his cell, Vahl turned slightly as he heard a key grate in the lock. His frame, thin when he reached Paris, was still nearer emaciation. He had been given nothing but bread and water since he had been imprisoned, and little of that. Neither had he been given any covering against the chill and damp of the unheated room. But he was not cold.

Fever throbbed in his blood, blotting out his present evil case and exposing him in his delirium once more to the terrors of his nightmare flight. But, hearing someone approach, he struggled to sit up.

"Is it time?" he asked breathlessly, as the bulky figure of his jailer appeared from behind the stout oak door.

"Not till sundown," growled the surly fellow, keeping his hand suggestively on the dagger at his belt as he lounged in the doorway. "The executioner has only begun to sharpen his axe. The King has sent you some company, that's all. You can say your prayers together before you die."

The tramp of men-at-arms sounded in the stone corridor. The jailer stepped back, and a new prisoner was thrust violently into the room. His gray eyes blinked in the dim light, since the small barred slit in the wall let in none of the dazzling sunshine outside. His face, which had always been stylishly clean-shaven, bore a mat of brown bristles; his chestnut hair had become threaded with gray. A wretched homespun mantle half hid, half exposed cote-hardie and hose torn and covered with dirt. Even so changed, Vahl knew him.

"Sir Olivier! Why are you here?"

The tall aristocrat stared, stepped forward swiftly, and grasped the youth's shoulder. "Is it the young falconer?" he marvelled. "You look like a ghost!"

82

"He will be one, soon enough," chuckled the coarse voice of the jailer. The knight turned on him with such a look of fury that the man hastily backed out the door, slammed it behind him, and shot the bolt, before he took time to turn the key. "And you both deserve what you get, you lying, traitorous deserters!" he shouted from the safety of the hall as he swaggered away.

"So they did not believe you, either?" questioned Vahl bitterly.

"Not one word would the King hear!" growled the knight, pacing back and forth in the narrow cell. "I never guessed that the news had reached him. I knelt and prayed his forgiveness for bearing evil tidings; but when I told him the French knights had met Bajazet and been slaughtered almost to a man, he went into a rage. He swore his realm was infested with traitors and deserters, and I should die under the headsman's axe before the sun went down! He gave me a cruel welcome for a Christ's Mass Day after these months of hardship!"

"Where is Artur?" demanded Vahl, his hand stealing to his breast, where the garnet glove still lay concealed.

"I wish to God I knew," Artur's father answered. "I fear he is carrion for crows to pick, God rest his soul!"

"Might he not have escaped, since you did?" Vahl asked hopefully, pressing his cold hands against his hot forehead, trying to hold back the delirium which threatened him.

Gloomily Sir Olivier shook his head. "He stayed in camp to polish my armor while I went out with a foraging party on the morning of the battle. As we returned with our provisions, we met some runaways, who told us that the Turks had routed our army with great slaughter, and we must flee to save ourselves. I had a good score of men-at-arms with me, and we had no mind for flight; but as we rode forward to the battle, a horde of infidels bore down upon us. We stood them off, though both sides lost good men in the fray. But seeing their numbers, we retreated as best we could. I could not get back to Artur, but I know he must have fallen, for he longed to be in the forefront of the battle."

"I grieve with you," said Vahl very low. "I had hoped for other tidings." He laid the dusty glove in Sir Olivier's hand.

"Where did you get that?" asked the knight, staring.

"From a Turkish looter," Vahl answered.

Tears came into Sir Olivier's eyes, and he made the sign of the cross. "Hope, then, is vain," he muttered. Silently he stroked the velvet gauntlet until Vahl roused him with another question.

"How did you win to safety?"

"Two companions and I came home through Wallachia, where the people pretended friendship for us, and then robbed us of all our possessions — clothing, arms, and mounts — so that we suffered from cold and hunger. Only the kindness of the good people of Vienna, who gave us cloaks to cover us and food for our hunger, gave us strength to finish our journey."

"But if you have companions," puzzled Vahl, "how can the King fail to believe your story? Surely you all tell the same tale?"

"My men will back me up if they hear of my plight," said Sir Olivier. "But when we reached the gates of Paris, I sent them both to their homes and made my way alone to court. It may be they will learn nothing until too late." He paced to the embrasure in the wall and tried to look out the narrow opening. "There is little time before the sun sets for them to persuade His stubborn Majesty that we spoke truth."

"Surely," said the boy hopefully, "the King will never send us to our death unshriven, and no priest has visited me in the three days I have been here."

"That madman may do any misdeed," muttered the knight in his beard. He stopped his pacing and confronted his young companion. "Three days, you say, young falconer? My fellows and I made what speed we could, yet you say you outstripped us. How was that?"

"I fled into the hills, rather than toward the river," Vahl explained. "I still had the Greenland falcon, and I had a horse. Those two saved my life many times over. The bird killed game, which she and I ate raw while the horse grazed. We outdistanced you, very likely, because we did not need to beg, and we trusted trees and rocks more for our shelter than we trusted strangers."

"You three—horse, bird, and boy—all reached Paris in safety?" queried the older man.

"Aye, and straight to the court of Philip of Burgundy we went. Traitor and deserter the Duke branded me unheard, and here I have starved for three days in prison, until now I must die."

Knight and squire both fell silent. The hopeful crusade which had led so many of their companions to death was now leading them to the same bitter end.

The clanking of arms in the corridor startled Vahl to life. He ran to the narrow window; the sun still shone. Yet the steps approached their door. The bolt was shot and the key turned; a gray-robed priest stepped quietly into the room.

"Father Matthieu!" cried Vahl, relief shining in his face as he recognized the chaplain of the Hôtel d'Artois. "Has Duke Philip sent you to release us?"

"I come to shrive your souls," replied the dean of the Duke's chapel, turning pitying eyes from one to the other of the prisoners.

"Holy father," asked the knight sternly, "do you know of what we are accused?"

"I do, my son," the priest answered gently.

"Then, even if you doubt our news, you know it may be true. I swear to you by the Holy Cross, father, it is true. It will be confirmed to the King's shame after we are dead. When I entered Paris there were two trusty squires with me. Seek them, I beg you, while there is time.

The priest's hands trembled. He clasped them about the wooden cross which hung from his girdle. "Your men heard of your imprisonment and went to court," he said. "They were marched past your door when I entered. While you go to the headsman's block, they are to be drowned in the Seine."

Vahl sank back against the wall; the knight paced back and forth fighting for self-control in his fury at the injustice.

The priest steeled himself against pity, and inflicted another wound.

"I fear you will have another companion also. As I came here with your squires, to give them what comfort I could, one broke from his guards on the way and dashed into the tavern, shouting at a travel-stained knight inside. They were both seized, and the knight dragged off to court."

"Could not the King wait for confirmation of our news?" demanded Sir Olivier, staring at the priest as if for hope. Father Matthieu only fixed his gaze dumbly on the ground. Sir Olivier's shoulders sagged. At last he spoke, very low.

"God forgive us all our sins!"

"Amen!" replied the priest, and bade the two prisoners kneel down with him and join in the prayers for the dying.

But the sacred rite was interrupted by another tramp of armed men in the corridor. Harsh voices called to the prisoners to come out. The priest went before, exhorting them to join in the prayers he repeated. Another group of guards brought Sir Olivier's squires, chained, behind them.

A headsman's block stood in the courtyard of the Châtelet, but the procession did not halt. It passed out the gate toward the river, between the two round towers of stone. Vahl paid little attention. Weakened by fever, he could hardly summon strength for setting one foot before another, and he wanted to show a bravery he could not feel. His companion pinched him to awareness, muttering in his ear:

"They are taking us all to the Grève to be drowned! That is the justice of an insane monarch!"

But they passed by the Grève, with its pillory and its whipping post, its gallows and the wooden tower on the sandy shore from which the weighted bodies of condemned criminals were thrown into the Seine. They followed the river bank past the walls of the inner city until they stood at the gates of the Hôtel de Saint Pol where the King of France held court.

"Pass in at once," ordered the guards, and the cheerless procession entered. Wonder filled Vahl's mind. Sir Olivier's face, and Father Matthieu's, too, showed that they shared his puzzlement.

Waiting ushers conducted them into the great hall. They stood before their King, dazzled by the splendor of the richest court in Christendom.

Vahl had seen state councils of the kings of Austria and Hungary, but the two together would not have provided the lavish display surrounding Charles VI. The knights and ladies, in their trailing robes, brocaded in rich colors and crested with gold embroidery, girt with gold and decked with jewels, blazed with color. In all the throng Charles and Queen Isabeau alone were seated. They sat on their dais in golden chairs, with golden crowns upon their heads. The strange fashion of the Queen's taffeta gown caught Vahl's eye: the right half was blue, embroidered with the arms of her husband; and the left half white, with the arms of her father, Duke Stephen of Bavaria.

The young monarch rose from his throne as the prisoners were led to his feet. It was one of His Majesty's good days; he gave no sign of the madness which so often racked him. He was richly clothed in a blue robe powdered with the gold fleur-de-lis of France. Philip of Burgundy stood beside him garbed in cloth of gold. In both uncle and nephew the long hooked nose, the wide but receding forehead and chin, the thin lips and ice-blue eyes spoke of their near kinship.

With fitting majesty the King spoke.

"You are my free and loyal men. The guards may go!"

The prisoners knelt stupefied before him. A knight richly clad but shabby from long travel, his skin burned brown, stepped from the gay ranks of the courtiers and knelt with them.

"Let me thank you for us all, your Majesty!"

With a thrill of recognition, Vahl stared. Sir James de Helly!

"We accept your thanks," said the King graciously. "But we, too, owe them. We will pay our debt. We would have slain these faithful servants had you not saved them. Sirs, you came with rumors unconfirmed, and we could not credit them. Sir James de Helly came accredited as the Emperor Bajazet's ambassador, bringing word of our faithful henchmen basely murdered and of the sad plight of the worthy gentlemen held for ransom. Now, to repay you for your imprisonment, let each man ask some boon, and it shall be granted if it lies in our royal power."

"My Lord and King," said Sir Olivier, speaking first as became his rank, "grant, then, that I may help to rescue my comrades from Bajazet!"

"That is a right loyal and knightly boon," said the pleased monarch. "But how could it be done?

Bajazet has taken his army and his prisoners to the
city of Bursa, where we cannot attack him. All
that remains for us is to raise the ransom he requires.

"Sire, it can be done!" cried Philip of Burgundy at the king's right hand. "Consider the ransom demands which Sir James brought from the
Sultan! The scarlet cloth, the tapestries, the fine
linens he asks for, money will buy. Money we have.
But Bajazet also demands twelve Greenland falcons!
Twelve Greenland falcons! I doubt if there are
that many in all Europe! I have one; your Majesty
has one; but I know of no others. Doubtless Bajazet
set the number, asking for the impossible. But for
the sake of my son and his men, the impossible must
be accomplished!"

"Sir Olivier," asked King Charles, "if a ship
were fitted out for a voyage to Greenland under your
command, to seek and bring back white falcons,
would you still ask for your first boon, or another?"

"Though the icebergs of Greenland were as ab-
horrent to me as the fires of hell," said the knight
soberly, "I would remember the plight of my comrades, and I would still ask to go to Greenland!"

"And my boon is: let me go with him!" Vahl
cried. "I know the lore of the birds and will care
for them well!"

"That he could do," vowed Sir James de Helly.
"The birds in his care provided many of your son's
friends with excellent sport on the crusade, my lord

Philip. It is a pity that John of Nevers' Greenland falcon was lost — or, more likely, Bajazet has it. Probably that is the bird which has fired his desire."

"That is the bird, but Bajazet does not have it, my lord," Vahl said quietly. "It rode on my wrist and fed me with its prey on my long journey."

"Where is it now?" asked Philip of Burgundy, his heavy brows knitting into a deep frown.

"It was in your mews, my lord Philip, when I was rushed off to prison. I cannot tell further," Vahl answered. He was beginning to feel dizzy.

"If you speak truth," vowed the Duke, "you shall be a falconer to my House as long as you desire, whether you outlive your usefulness or not." He gave quick orders to a squire, who hurried out.

"Sir Olivier will need to bring back only eleven falcons; I can vouch for that," said Sir James.

"If it prove so, this falconer shall indeed go with Sir Olivier to Greenland," promised the king. "Now, what boon shall we grant to these other two worthy men? We are pleased with the loyalty of our unselfish servants," purred Charles, whose extravagance regarding the expenses of his own household was only equalled by his parsimony elsewhere. "We feel sure that these, no less than the others, are concerned for their fellows more than for themselves."

The two men-at-arms whispered together briefly, and the braver spoke: "Your Majesty is right, as always, Sire. We do desire the welfare of our comrades, and our boons are these. Let the ambassador who goes to Bajazet promise him twelve falcons, and let him carry with him the first three: the falcon of the Count of Nevers, the falcon of the Duke of Burgundy, and the falcon of our lord King Charles."

"Your boons are granted. You may go," ordered the king ungraciously, for he had been fairly caught. The squires retreated from his presence, but Duke Philip stopped them.

"It shall never be said of Philip of Burgundy that he let generosity to his son go unrewarded!" he cried, throwing them his purse. The coins in it chinked pleasantly in the squires' ears as they bowed themselves out.

"My lord," said the Duke's messenger, returning, "the falcon of the Count of Nevers is safe at your chateau."

"And so shall you be, Sir Olivier and my young henchman, until your ship be fitted out to sail!" proclaimed the Duke, extending his hands to raise them to their feet, since all this time they had remained on their knees before the King.

But young Vahl's blood beat in his veins like liquid fire. Weak from fever, hunger, and the relief of reprieve from death, he stretched out his hand to his patron's. He was not strong enough to clasp it. He fainted at the King's feet.

6

Delay

OR DAYS VAHL lay delirious, raving wildly of his comrades and their fate in Turkey. The court physician probed his festering wound, and found a sliver of metal embedded in the flesh. The splinter came out with a gush of blood, leaving the weak invalid still weaker.

When Vahl came to his senses, he found himself stripped of his travel-worn garments, and his painful right shoulder bandaged with sweet-smelling balm. He lay in a featherbed between sheets of fine linen, covered with blankets of soft wool. As he opened his eyes to the fire blazing on the hearth, the tapestried room seemed to him very like Paradise.

Beside the fire, with a hank of clean-washed wool and her wooden cards, sat Dame Louise, busily stretching out a fine thread on her twirling spindle.

This waiting woman to Duchess Marguerite was the one Vahl liked the best of all the castle folk in the Hôtel d'Artois. She was a Fleming who had come with her mistress from Flanders when the great lady was wed to Duke Philip, and had attended her ever since. The court held her in high regard, for she was skilled in the use of herbs and in the care of the sick. It was she who had helped to care for Vahl's father, Thorfinn, before he died, and more than one cut finger had she bound up for Vahl Thorfinnsson when he was a little lad. Vahl smiled at her.

Feeling his gaze, Dame Louise looked up from her spinning. She brushed back a tiny dark curl that had escaped from her snowy coif. Her brown eyes were kind, and her face unlined by any wrinkles except two small ones which had replaced dimples in her cheeks. Seeing that Vahl was awake, she laid her wool aside.

"Drink this," she bade him, bringing a copper mug from a trivet on the hearth. He gulped the broth greedily.

"Slowly, slowly!" she admonished.

"It is good!" Vahl mumbled. The hot liquid seemed to clear his foggy brain.

"I thought it was only food you needed," said Dame Louise with satisfaction as he drained the cup. "If you had not come to yourself soon, the leech would have bled you again, the silly fool!"

"Dame Louise," asked Vahl curiously, "why am I here instead of in the falconers' quarters?"

" 'The laborer is worthy of his hire,' " quoted the lady piously. "Did not you, in the face of danger, secure for Duke Philip one-twelfth of his son's ransom?"

"But I deserve little thanks for that," Vahl said. "The bird and I saved each other."

"Then enjoy the gratitude that is heaped upon you all the more," advised his nurse cheerfully. "You will do plenty of good deeds that get no thanks, so make hay while the sun shines."

"So your patient is out of his stupor?" asked Sir Olivier from the door. The knight was freshly shaven, bathed and perfumed, and clad in a long olive-green silk robe which reached to his pointed velvet shoes. He seated himself beside Vahl on the massive carved bed. "I began to fear that I must be off to Greenland without you."

"No, no!" cried Vahl, struggling to sit up again and throwing off his coverings. "I can go at once. I am strong enough —"

"Lie down! Lie down!" shrieked Dame Louise from the hearth. "At your peril you stir out of that bed!" She scurried toward him and tucked him in once more. "A fine nurse you would make, Sir Olivier!" she scolded. "First you bid me cherish him like your own son, and then you come in and stir him out of bed like this —"

96

"I only meant to tease him," laughed the man. "I could not be off to Greenland yet even if I wished."

"Why?" Vahl asked. "Surely the Duke knows that delay may mean evil for the prisoners in Turkey?"

"He knows," Sir Olivier nodded. "He was for sending us off in a Paris ship the instant you could set one foot before another. But when he called in the city merchants, it appeared that not one could provide vessel, captain, or crew able to find the way to Greenland. Worse still, they could not say what other hanse was better fitted. But the ambassador of the Hanseatic League told Duke Philip that knowledge to fit his need could be had at the League office in Bruges. Until word comes back, there is nothing we can do. So lie still, lad, and get back your strength."

He patted the invalid's good shoulder clumsily, and bowed in courtly fashion to Dame Louise as he left. Vahl watched restlessly for his return next day, a question on the tip of his tongue.

"Will Sir James de Helly go with us to Greenland?"

"He cannot," Sir Olivier answered. "He is not a free man like us, remember. He is Bajazet's ambassador, sent here to demand ransom for the captive knights. The Sultan released him only on his word of honor to return at once."

"What news has he of our comrades?"

"None that is meat for a sick stomach," said Sir Olivier. "Of all our company, not more than two score remain alive. The others were all massacred, as not likely to bring sufficient ransom to make them worth keeping."

"The Hungarians and their allies also, as well as the French?" asked Vahl, horror-struck.

"No; at least not in such numbers," said Sir Olivier bitterly. "It seems that the French knights insisted on advancing against the Turks when Sir James first brought news of their approach without even waiting to learn what force the infidels had. They dashed out against the express commands of Sigismond, before the Hungarians had made ready their army. When the French were routed, their retreat stampeded the other troops. Sigismond and some of his knights and men escaped across the Danube, blaming the French for their defeat. They have vowed never to send one single soldier or coin to rescue the survivors. John of Nevers sent word to his father by James de Helly to agree to any demands that Bajazet might make. John feared that unless his father took the Sultan's first offer, the Turk would never make another."

"Then can nothing be done to aid our people before we bring back the birds from Greenland?" worried Vahl.

"Much is being done," said the knight more

98

cheerfully. "All that Bajazet demands, apart from the falcons, is to be sent him at once."

"But falcons!" Vahl persisted. "Are there no more to be found in Europe?"

"Duke Philip knows of none, but he has sent a message to every prince in Christendom, offering to pay any price if a Greenland hawk is to be had."

"The father of the Duchess of Orleans has two!" Vahl sat upright in his eagerness to tell good news.

Sir Olivier stared at him. "How do you know that?"

"I heard her say so, before ever we went on the crusade."

"She has not mentioned the fact to Duke Philip," said Sir Olivier wryly. "Of course, the birds may be dead —"

"A Greenland falcon should live a dozen years, or even a score," Vahl protested. "Surely both have not died, and surely Duke Philip should be able to get one. Even one would help pay the ransom."

"Possibly the Duke of Milan does not feel helpful," suggested Sir Olivier.

"No Christian prince could feel otherwise!" cried Vahl.

"Do you consider Gian Galeazzo Visconti a Christian prince?" asked Sir Olivier sarcastically.

"I know nothing at all about him. I never heard his name before. Why do you speak as if he is a monster?" queried Vahl, lying back weakly.

"In Italy we call him 'the viper' — and it is not only because a viper is his blazon. Forgive me, boy; I supposed you knew the common gossip about his misdeeds. Of course you have not heard the latest news of him."

"From your tone, it must be evil," said Vahl.

"Evil it is. When Bajazet sent James de Helly here, he bade him return from France to Turkey by way of Milan, where he should thank Bajazet's good friend, Gian Galeazzo, for keeping him informed of the progress of the Christian crusade!"

"Are you telling me," demanded Vahl incredulously, "that the Duke of Milan betrayed the crusaders to their foes?"

Sir Olivier nodded. "That much we know to be true. We suspect even more. Sir James says that when the French knights were captured, Bajazet already knew their names and titles. He knew exactly which to spare in order to demand the highest ransom for the fewest prisoners. Who could have told him better than his 'good friend' in Milan?"

"Horrible!" whispered Vahl. He shut his eyes. Suddenly he remembered something. That dark foreigner who had ridden by in the retinue of the Duchess of Orleans while he waited on the hill of Montmartre for the march east to begin was the same swarthy Italian who had laughed heartily with Bajazet over the destruction of the Christian host. Vahl understood now how the knight had come to be in Turkey. He opened his eyes. "Horrible! And yet — I know that it is true!"

"How?" demanded Sir Olivier sharply. Vahl told him. The knight was silent for awhile.

"Well, it is the nature of a viper to strike. Yet in justice I must say that even a viper, trodden on, has a right to defend itself. I had not known before that the French princes had thought of attacking Gian Galeazzo, but I can well believe it. His provinces are rich, and his French brother-in-law does not like powerful neighbors."

"Brother-in-law?" repeated Vahl, puzzled.

"Aye. Gian Galeazzo is married to Duke Philip's sister. There is no rivalry more bitter than in a quarrelsome family; no devotion greater than in a loving one. Perhaps Duke Philip can heal the breach and win a little devotion. I will speak to him about the birds."

Three days later Sir Olivier, entering the sickroom, found the invalid propped with pillows. He was finishing a trencher meal of enormous proportions, and demanding to be allowed out of bed.

"I shall be ready to start for Greenland the very instant that word comes from Bruges," Vahl boasted at sight of him.

"The rascal is still as weak as a newborn babe," Dame Louise protested. "Yet he maintains he is a husky oaf, and will have no more of me."

"Keep him under your thumb until he has his

strength," smiled Sir Olivier. "Word has come from Bruges, but we cannot start yet."

"Why?" cried Vahl.

"It seems that a king of Norway, who governed the country of Greenland, long since sold all its trade to the merchants of the North German Hanseatic League. The Hanse sends but one ship each year to visit the people. We must wait for that ship."

"Until when?"

"It sails from Bergen, in Norway, next June," Sir Olivier told him.

Vahl almost wailed. "Bajazet may not spare his prisoners that long!"

"Sir John de Chateaumorant will bear him the three falcons in France to whet his appetite, and Duke Philip is commissioning Sir James de Helly to obtain the Duke of Milan's birds if he can, on his way to Turkey. Those two knights must convince Bajazet that the other birds will be sent."

"Surely," Vahl suggested, "Duke Philip would gladly charter a ship of his own to make the voyage earlier."

"Even Duke Philip cannot rule the seasons," the older man explained. "The ship sails in summer because only then are the fiords of Greenland open water. Nine months of the year, and sometimes more, they are ice-locked, and no ship can approach them."

"I see." Vahl sighed. After a moment's thought he spoke again.

"Lord Olivier, I am almost well now, and I cannot stay here much longer. It is a long time until June. Will you go to Pierre the falconer for me, and inquire if I may return to my work with him?"

Sir Olivier took a turn about the room before he spoke. "If you so wish, I will speak to Pierre. A place is waiting for you, by the Duke's order, though Pierre's brother has been helping him since you left. But if you will, since you are to go with me to Norway, I will take you into my service and train you in knightly ways."

"It is not hard to choose!" gasped Vahl, his blue eyes sparkling. "I will be your man — your true and loyal man — Sir Olivier!"

"So be it!" said the knight warmly. His voice sounded husky. He turned and went out, but not before Vahl had caught the glitter of tears in his gray eyes.

"He never ceases mourning for his son," said Dame Louise in a low voice as the door closed behind him. "Without you to think of, he would be desolate indeed."

"I cannot take Artur's place," said Vahl sadly.

"Sir Olivier means that you shall," said the lady. "See what he had me hide here against the day when you will be up and dressed again."

103

From a carved chest of oak in the corner of the room she drew out a suit of garnet color, complete from hood to hose. Except that it bore no gold-embroidered crest, it was like that in which Vahl had first seen Artur, and which Artur had so often worn at banquets on the crusade. Vahl felt a lump rise in his throat as he looked at it.

"I will try to wear it with honor," he whispered.

Dame Louise smiled at him. Hastily she returned the rich robe to the chest. Vahl wondered why she turned her back on him with such speed; she seemed to be dabbling furtively at her eyes.

When once Dame Louise pronounced him well enough for visitors, Vahl did not suffer from loneliness. The Duchess of Burgundy, Marguerite of Flanders herself, came to hear his account of the crusade. For several days the young Countess of Nevers, Marguerite of Hainault, slipped in each afternoon, leading her two children, to ask countless questions about the doings of her husband. The waiting women and castle maids hung in the background, their eyes widening at tales of the fearful Turks. One maid in particular Vahl always watched for. The long braids of dark hair coiled about her ears framed a delicate face which changed with his every word: sympathy, approval, horror, and joy were mirrored in her wide dark eyes, and replaced each other quickly. He never had speech with her alone, but Dame Louise told him that her father was one of the knights known to have been slain at Nicopolis. Her name was Jeannette de la Puys. Her mother, too, had died during the crusade; her only sister was married to a Norwegian knight in Bergen. She had asked for and been granted permission to travel there with Sir Olivier and Vahl.

When at last Vahl was well enough to wait on Sir Olivier at meat in the great hall, he dressed with care in his new garnet robe. He was struggling desperately to fasten the points of his long hose when Sir Olivier came to his rescue.

"I am used to long hose," said Vahl in excuse, "but mine have always been loose and baggy, and not so stylish in fit as these."

"Why not say skintight, and shame the Devil with the truth?" asked Sir Olivier, chuckling, as he made the points firm and helped to lace on the tight tunic. "Have you never noticed with what erectness courtiers always bear themselves?"

"Yes," said Vahl wistfully. "I will try to bear myself so, Sir Olivier, to do you proper honor, but I cannot promise to succeed."

"You cannot do otherwise," laughed the knight. "Do you think such carriage is an accident of birth? Try bending your back in this stiff jacket I have just laced on you, and you will soon see otherwise! And walk with care until you are used to these pointed shoon. It is not for nothing we all go goose-stepping around the court; it is to keep our tight hose unwrinkled and the long points of our shoes from getting underfoot and tripping us! Some day I am going to follow the ladies' example, and hold up my shoe points with silver chains to my belt!''

"The falcons would not know me in this gay plumage," said Vahl, fastening his sleeves at the wrist and surveying his rich garb with awe.

"The courtiers will know you better," said the knight dryly, "and it is they with whom you will associate now."

"Sir Olivier," said Vahl hesitantly, "I — I am more used to the ways of a mews than of a court."

"Perhaps that is why I am so fond of you," answered Sir Olivier with some irony. "Your manners are so much better than those I often see around me." Grinning, he gave the squire a resounding clap on the back. "We have been through much together," he said. "God willing, perhaps we may continue to survive fate's onslaughts! Come!"

A few days later, a messenger reached the palace of Burgundy with a letter from Sir James de Helly in Lombardy. The Duke of Milan, he wrote, refused to part with his Greenland hawks, either for Christian love or money.

"The Duke declares," wrote Sir James, "that he has before this given his dear friend Bajazet several Iceland falcons, and he knows his gift must have pleased the Sultan or he would not be so eager for kindred birds from Greenland. Therefore he will indeed send Bajazet one of his birds if Duke Philip fails to raise the ransom number. But if so, the bird will be a free gift from friend to friend and no part of the ransom. As for the other falcon, the Duke is devoted to it himself, and he asserts that Bajazet would never consent to his robbing himself of his own good sport."

"The fiend!" cried Vahl when he heard this. "I wondered how Bajazet's Iceland falcons came so far south!"

The Duke of Milan's message roused great anger in France and Burgundy, for both courts had lost many worthy gentlemen in the crusade. Knights begged Duke Philip to lead an army against Milan, or to seize the Duke of Milan's daughter, the Duchess of Orleans, and use her against her father. But he was a clever man, and he did not allow his first fury to drive him to rashness. It was not fear of "the viper" that held Philip back, but fear for his son's safety. He reasoned that if he went to war against Milan, or if harm came to the Duke of Milan's daughter, the Italian prince might persuade Bajazet to slaughter all his French prisoners as a personal favor. Therefore the Duke of Burgundy held his hand and curbed his followers, though it cost his proud spirit many bitter hours. Nor did it help that his messengers returned from the courts of the kings of Europe, their hands empty of falcons.

7

The Quest Begins

N March the Council of the Hanseatic League in Bruges sent word to Duke Philip that his emissaries should take ship from Bruges to Bergen in early May. In mid-April the impatient Duke bade Sir Olivier and Vahl set out.

One early morning, Sir Olivier and Vahl knelt with the Duke's household in the chapel to hear Mass sung for the success of their mission. Then, with the young girl who was to accompany them, they mounted their waiting horses in the courtyard. Courtiers and henchmen gathered around to wish them Godspeed. Among them all, not one — not even travelled knight or learned priest — knew anything about Greenland except that it lay far over the ocean west of Iceland. They felt sure it must be upon the very edge of the world, and fearful were they for the knight and squire who must sail there. Dame Louise, with tears in her eyes, pressed upon each a little silver reliquary containing a finger-joint of a holy martyr, on a silver chain. Sir Olivier insisted that she herself should hang the costly gift about his neck to protect him from evil. He kissed it before he tucked it safely beneath his tunic, and his eyes dwelt long on hers.

The two Marguerites gave to Vahl a heavy fur-lined cloak of wool for his journey, and a fine silver belt and mantle-brooch in gratitude for his service to their son and husband. Duke Philip gave to both knight and squire well-filled purses for their personal needs, and to Sir Olivier a letter of credit to any and all representatives of the Hanseatic League, bought at a great price by the Duke from the League's ambassador in Paris. Then Philip himself led his retinue with them to the courtyard gate to wave a last farewell.

They had expected to ride north alone; instead, they were accompanied by a score of mounted soldiers. Only the day before a messenger had brought word that a band of highwaymen were busy in South Flanders, and as yet the justice of the towns had not been able to catch up with their swift-moving robberies, so Duke Philip had chosen this troop to help capture the band. They were a gay and gallant company. Time passed swiftly for Vahl and Jeannette; and Sir Olivier relieved their weariness, when they rested, by chanting romantic lays to tunes on the harp which Vahl carried for him.

The highway they followed was one of the best in France. It had been used by the Romans and perhaps even long before their day. Countless people passed on it, of all classes, high or low, unarmed and apparently unafraid. They seemed to Vahl of a better spirit than the folk he had watched on the crusade to the east.

"You have a quick eye," agreed the knight with approval. "This is richer, freer country, and it has been lucky enough to have peace for some years. The cities of Flanders are the center of wool-weaving for the whole world, growing larger and wealthier every year."

"If all the country is like this," ventured Jeannette de la Puys timidly, looking at the peaceful landscape, "how can highwaymen ever hide themselves?"

"This country is as wild as any other, off the beaten track," said Sir Olivier. "There are still great stretches of forest land, though they are growing smaller. But fear not, lass; we shall stay on the guarded ways."

So they did, resting at a great monastery the first night and at a manor house the second. On the third day they reached Saint Quentin, at the crossing of five old military roads. There the Duke's troops learned that the highwaymen had waylaid three travellers on a byroad to the west the day previous. So they bade farewell to Sir Olivier and the young people, and galloped away on their own errand. The three travelled that day to the castle of an old friend of Sir Olivier's, where they feasted until late. But early they were off again, taking a rougher but shorter road than that through Lille. It was wilder country than Sir Olivier expected, and they met almost no travellers. He grew increasingly watchful, but saw nothing at all to cause him concern.

When the sun was high and hot, the travellers found a pleasant picnic place with a mossy brook on one side and a cool wood on the other. They turned their horses out to graze and drink while they ate bread and cheese in the shade of an oak. Sir Olivier tuned his harp.

"If all wayfaring is as pleasant as this," said Jeannette, "I wonder that anyone can bear to be cooped up inside four walls when summer comes."

A twig suddenly crackled in the underbrush behind her. "Keep on talking!" Sir Olivier bade her in a quick undertone, strumming loud chords and gazing intently toward the wood.

"What is it?" she whispered instead.

"Do you know the Lay of the Court that went Maying?" asked Sir Olivier in a jovial shout, stretching, and hissing under his breath, "A man! Nay, two! Get between me and the tree! Cursed be my carelessness in letting the horses stray!"

"I'll bring some water, and you shall sing it," Vahl said loudly, jumping to his feet. He added, low, "I'll get the horses."

"Stand!" yelled a harsh voice. "Don't move, or I'll shoot!"

Vahl broke into a wild run. An arrow whistled, and quivered in the ground ahead of him. He leaped into the saddle of the nearest horse — Sir Olivier's — and galloped the animal toward his own mount. Seizing its reins, he bore back toward the picnickers. Another arrow zoomed uncomfortably close. Sir Olivier had placed Jeannette behind him against the tree-trunk, and stood, harp in hand, watching three ruffians armed with bows, arrows ready to the string, advancing toward him.

"Around the tree, Jeannette!" Vahl shouted. The trunk screened them for a second as the girl swung up on the other horse. "Ride out of bow-shot," he called to her, scarcely checking his speed as he galloped toward the woods to bear down on the bowmen from behind.

His wild rush carried him into a hornet's nest, for two more horsemen were watching events from the shadowy undergrowth, guarding three riderless horses evidently belonging to the bowmen. One of the horsemen, a black-bearded giant, drew his sword at sight of Vahl and rushed toward him.

Between them stood one of the riderless horses. Vahl struck it on the flank with the flat of his sword as he went by. The beast reared and plunged headlong to one side, careening into the second horseman, a red-bearded villain with a deep scar on his right cheek. The man's mount reared and threw him. Those two horses disappeared into the woods, branches snapping with their passage. The other two wandered out to the highway, where one of the bowmen, leaving his two companions to threaten Sir Olivier, chased them.

Blackbeard and Vahl set to with their swords, thrusting and parrying with all their skill. Vahl was hard pressed, for under his tunic his opponent wore a shirt of chain mail, off which the blows slid harmlessly. Yet Vahl soon knew himself to be the better swordsman; the wild blows of the other could not pierce his guard. He struck the fellow's weapon from his hand, just in time to meet a charge from the unhorsed Redbeard, whom he wounded in his sword arm. Redbeard's blade would have dropped from his hand had not the black-bearded giant horseman seized it and renewed the fray. The wounded man sought a dagger in his belt with his left hand, and Vahl gave ground, so that the trampling feet of the circling horses kept him safe a few seconds. Once more he struck Blackbeard's sword from his hand, but still he could not wound him.

Jeannette shrieked piercingly from the highway, and Vahl rushed toward the sound. The third bowman had caught a horse, overtaken her, and was binding her arms behind her with leathern thongs. He turned as Vahl shouted, seized his bow and shot; but the arrow went wild. He drew his sword. Vahl rushed at him, hoping to finish him off before Blackbeard could come up to them. Blackbeard, however, did not join the fight; he shouted to his henchman as he came up, "You have him!" seized the helpless girl's bridle rein, and led her horse beside his own back toward the forest.

He reckoned without Sir Olivier. While one bowman had kept him in close range with an arrow aimed at the knight's heart, the second had gone forward to bind his arms. When his would-be captor stepped within arms' reach Sir Olivier threw his harp full-force in the man's face, whipped out his sword and cut him down. Instantly an arrow struck him in the upper left arm; astonishment had made the bowman's sight waver, or the wound might have been fatal. Before the man could shoot again, the knight plucked out the arrow and attacked him with uplifted sword. As the terrified bowman fled before him, the knight shouted his war cry.

Pursuit was hopeless through the trees, but Sir Olivier found one of the riderless horses and sprang into the saddle in time to see the girl being dragged into the wood. Blackbeard, encumbered by two horses, was delayed long enough for Sir Olivier to reach him. Furiously they hacked at each other. While they sweated and panted, the wounded

Redbeard and the fleeing bowman recovered their wits and their horses. Instead of joining their fighting comrades, they seized the girl's horse. This time it was Redbeard who led her away.

On the hitherto deserted highway, horses' hoofs began to thud. Voices shouted faintly in the distance. The marauders tried to flee from their opponents, but Vahl and Sir Olivier pressed them too closely. Up came half a score of the Burgundian men-at-arms and speedily ended the battle. They seized the highwaymen and trussed them securely. The Burgundian leader dispatched half a dozen men after the captive girl, who was recovered, after a hard chase, along with her captors.

"You came just in time to save us!" Sir Olivier said to the Burgundians, gloomily kicking his shattered harp.

"Lucky we did," their captain told him soberly. "It was only chance."

He refused to leave the place until he was sure that all the ruffians were accounted for. The first bowman Sir Olivier had engaged was dead; the others were bound with their feet beneath their horses' bellies, and taken to court at Lille. Since Sir Olivier's wound needed tending, the three travellers went back that far also. Once more a monastery gave Sir Olivier and his squire and ward housing and food. A skilled monk washed Sir Olivier's wound and bound it with healing herbs.

A good night's rest restored the spirits of the weary and frightened girl. When the travellers set out again for Bruges, she rode as gaily as ever.

"Never had a maiden braver champions," said she proudly.

"It was not we who won the final victory," Sir Olivier reminded her.

"You would have won it if the soldiers had not interrupted," said Jeannette loyally. Sir Olivier chided her for ingratitude to the Burgundians, but her words pleased him and Vahl. Their journey to Bruges passed very pleasantly.

Within the walls of Bruges lay one of the busiest cities of the world. Just as Venice dominated the trade of the Mediterranean, so Bruges commanded the trade of the north.

The Duke of Burgundy maintained a great house there for his use when he came to visit his dominions in Flanders. Pompous Sir Julian, the seneschal, made the travellers welcome. He told them that many ships were in port, and that one, the *Man of Ghent,* was bound straight for Bergen. Northward passage for Sir Olivier's party was quickly arranged for the next day.

Sir Julian would have taken the three to a banquet in the town hall, where the wool-dyers were celebrating the name-day of their patron saint, but they preferred to see the city. The guildsmen were putting on pageants in wagons in the streets, and hundreds of townspeople were out to gape at them and at the city dignitaries in their rich robes entering the magnificent building. The markets were full of strange people and strange wares. Sir Olivier searched determinedly until he found a fine Italian lute, very rich and sweet in tone, to replace his broken harp. Vahl bought a new dagger of fine Damascus steel. Jeannette set her heart on a Little Lady — a life-size costume doll looking for all the world like Queen Isabeau in her parti-colored gown of blue and white. But the manikin was bought under her very nose by a richly dressed blond young man. When she saw the gold that changed hands, Jeannette was quite content to buy instead a length of finest rose damask to take to her sister.

Melodious chimes sounded the curfew hour all too soon, sending them to the Duke's chateau for sleep. Early next morning, the three travellers attended early Mass in the cathedral of Saint Sauveur, praying for the safety and success of their perilous journey.

Bruges lay some distance from the sea. The waterways which made it a great inland port had once been natural, formed by the Zwyn River. The silting of the channels had made necessary the building of canals, which linked Bruges to open water by way of Zeebrugge and Blankenberghe. So the hundred oarsmen rowed the *Man of Ghent* through the low-lying countryside, and did not even hoist a sail until they reached the coast. Then the billowing sails caught the wind so strongly that the seamen seldom had to touch their oars.

The ship was long and low, with high prow and stern. A carved figure of a merchant of Ghent, from which the vessel took its name, ornamented the prow, which was fitted likewise with a spear for ramming in case of a sea fight. The single deck was piled with casks of wine lashed down with ropes to iron braces; bales of woolen goods were stowed in the hold. The ship's crew and soldiers generally slept, as well as worked, on deck; but they could take shelter below in wet weather, although between cargo and deck floor there was not room for them to stand up. The passengers — half a dozen besides Sir Olivier's party — had a high, small castle in the stern for their apartment. From the first hour, Hilda, the only other woman in the party, took Jeannette in charge and appropriated half of the divided room for the ladies' private use.

Sir Olivier and Vahl shared the other half with Hilda's husband, Siegfried of Bremen, a rich Hanseatic merchant; his son Heinrich, grave and rather self-important; their middle-aged deaf servant; Father Anselm, an angular Italian priest; and the blond young man who had bought the Little Lady. He made himself known to them as Frithiof of Bergen, a young Norwegian returning home after a year in Paris. Hearing him speak, Vahl recognized a northern accent. All the passengers and most of the crew spoke French, the world language of the day; but each nationality gave it an accent readily distinguishable.

The *Man of Ghent,* having a full cargo, good sailing weather, and ample provisions for the voyage, stopped at no wayside ports, though it sailed often within sight of land. So the passengers saw much of each other — but however much Heinrich and Frithiof saw of Jeannette, it was not enough. They followed her like faithful dogs at heel, as grateful for a kind word or smile as a hungry hound for a bone, and as jealous of each other's favors as one famished beast is when another is fed.

Seeing what was going on, Sir Siegfried asked Sir Olivier if Jeannette came of good family. Being assured that she did, he said no more. Sir Olivier was amused at Jeannette's coquetry, and teased her. Vahl was annoyed, until he found cause for secret laughter. Dame Hilda had recounted more than once that only a lord's daughter with a great dowry would do for her Heinrich; now she feared that her own words had given Jeannette designs upon him, and worried openly to anyone who would listen. But when she saw that Heinrich gained no preference over his rival, she seethed with indignation that his merits were not recognized.

"That girl would keep the Angel Gabriel at arm's length!" she complained bitterly to Vahl. "So far as I can tell, not one kiss has either of these fine lads had from her!"

When the passengers awoke one morning to see hundreds of fishing boats sailing toward them from the Norwegian coast, they knew they were near Bergen. By midday the ship had steered its course between the mountainous islands which shut in the harbor, and the smell of fish was everywhere. And ashore, the fish were everywhere: fresh, salted, and drying; in the boats, in the markets, and even spread in great piles on the ground. Yet the town was clean and bright.

All the travellers parted with many good wishes. Even the silent priest, weighted down with the great roll of parchment which he would never trust out of his hands, surprised Sir Olivier by saying gravely to him:

"I am happy that we are to meet again."

8

Bergen and a Bird

WHEN SIR OLIVIER and Vahl delivered Jeannette de la Puys safely into the care of her
kindred, they intended to bid her a pleasant farewell and go about their business.
But her sister and her sister's husband,
Dame Therese and Sir Anders, would by no means
allow this. They insisted that knight and squire
should be their honored guests while they stayed in
Bergen. This both were glad to do.

"Twelve Greenland falcons!" Sir Anders mused
over their errand. "That explains why the Hanseatic
governor tried to force Sir Lars to sell his bird!"

"Do you mean that there is a Greenland falcon
in Bergen?" cried Sir Olivier.

"I do indeed," replied Sir Anders.

"Then why could not the Hanse buy it for Duke
Philip? You have no prince here, and in every civil-

ized country only those of royal birth can possess such a bird!"

"I know," Sir Anders nodded. "This falcon was meant as a gift for our Queen, and I will tell you why it was not for sale. Sir Lars needed it.

"To understand this story you must know that Bergen is really two cities: the Norwegian and the Hanseatic Settlement. Each has its own laws, and sometimes that makes trouble. Sir Lars belongs to the Norwegian city. He is one of our noblest knights.

"The Hanse is supposed to be ruled by a council, but really one man holds the power — the governor. He is a German from Lübeck, who thinks the German race superior to all others. When his son Friedrich fell in love with Sir Lars's daughter Hilda, the governor forbade the match. Friedrich wedded Hilda in spite of his father. Then Friedrich suddenly disappeared. It did not take much guessing to know that his father was responsible.

"Hilda sickened with grief. Her young brother Karl went to the governor and begged him to bring Friedrich back. The governor laughed, and Karl struck him. The governor had the boy thrown in prison as a would-be murderer and swore he should never be released. Sir Lars begged for his son's freedom in vain. And no one but Queen Margaret herself has the power to override the governor's verdict within the gaarde walls."

"From what we in France hear of your Queen,"

interrupted Sir Olivier, "she is not one to sit inactive while one of her subjects is abused."

"True," agreed Sir Anders. "But, unfortunately, Sir Lars was out of her favor. He is one of those who believe that, under the Union of the Three Crowns, Denmark, Sweden, and Norway should each retain its own laws and customs. The Queen thinks otherwise, and gives no aid to those who oppose her. So Sir Lars could not ask her for help. He had no way to comfort his daughter, and she died.

"Then, two summers ago, Captain Gunnar returned from a voyage to Greenland, bringing with him a young falcon. He knew that Queen Margaret was supposed to make a visit to Norway very soon. Because Sir Lars was his friend, Captain Gunnar gave him the bird as a gift for the Queen. She loves hawking, and if anything could win back her favor, the falcon would. But she did not come to Norway then. She has not come yet.

"A few months ago Sir Lars' son, Karl, died in prison in the Hanseatic Settlement, leaving his father childless. But Sir Lars kept the bird, saying openly that when the Queen finally came, he would give it to her and ask that this governor be removed.

"It must have been about that time when your master inquired for any Greenland falcon he might buy. Suddenly the governor threatened to arrest Sir Lars unless he sold the bird at the Hanse's price.

"Every knight in Bergen protested. We vowed that if the governor made Sir Lars a prisoner in the Hanseatic Settlement, the governor would be a prisoner there himself. If he so much as stuck his crooked nose outside the gate, he would find every knight in Bergen waiting to strike him down. Since that day we have heard no more threats from him, and Sir Lars still has his bird."

"I can understand if he will not sell it," said Sir Olivier, "but we must buy it if we can. Can we visit him tomorrow?"

"Better interview the governor about your ship first," Sir Anders suggested. "I could transact this business for you, but I could not recall a ship that has sailed."

There the matter dropped for the time being, but it came up again that evening, when two parties of guests arrived at the house within a few moments of each other, to the embarrassment of all.

First came Frithiof, accompanied by his stout, richly garbed parents. The elders Sir Anders and Dame Therese welcomed as old friends, while their son whisked Jeannette into a corner and murmured hastily. The girl kept her eyes downcast, but Vahl saw that her cheeks began to flush very pink. Then the color faded as a servant escorted Heinrich and his parents into the room. His father was a little stiffer than usual, but Dame Hilda bore up bravely, though her eyes were red from weeping.

Each pair of parents stiffly requested, viewing the other with suspicion, that they might have private word with Sir Anders. Having heard what each couple had to say, Sir Anders returned with them to the rest of the company and spoke gravely to his sister-in-law.

"It appears that two offers of marriage are being made to you by these worthy gentlemen," he said. "If you favor either or none, you are free to speak."

Vahl expected to see Jeannette blush again. Instead, she paled, but her voice was steady. "Both these gentlemen do me great honor," she said, with more dignity than Vahl had ever seen in her. "But ere I wed, I have a debt of gratitude to pay to this knight and squire who brought me safely hither. They seek nine Greenland falcons, and I am told there is one in Bergen. Whoever shall fetch me that falcon for a gift to them, him will I wed. Otherwise I am for the Church!"

Sir Olivier hastily protested. "No, no, Jeannette! You owe us no such debt! I myself will buy the falcon if it can be bought."

"He who loves me will gladly do me this service," Jeannette insisted. The two young men declared likewise. Both families took themselves away.

"This is ill done, Jeannette!" Sir Olivier once more tried to reason with the girl. "I cannot suffer you to do this thing! Marriage is sacred! It is not to be decided by the purchase of a falcon!"

"Do not fear," said Jeannette, smiling shyly. "I know my mind in this matter."

Proof that she spoke truly was not long in coming. At dawn the next morning a great pounding on the street door roused the household. Hastily Vahl and Sir Olivier tumbled out of their warm eider-down featherbed, pulled on jackets and hose, and emerged from their sleeping cubicle to join the startled family.

On the threshold they found Frithiof, beside a sweating horse. The young man carried a Greenland falcon on his gloved fist.

"Come out, falconer, and take this prize!" Frithiof called to Vahl. "I bid you to come dance at my wedding, as I have just bidden Heinrich!"

"I will come with more pleasure than he, I vow!" Vahl chuckled, running out to stroke the hooded hawk.

"You minx!" said Sir Olivier to Jeannette. "You had some foreknowledge of this!"

Jeannette's laughter confirmed his guess. She confessed: "That I had. Frithiof told me on the boat that he had been sent for by his uncle, Sir Lars, whose son had just died. When I heard my brother-in-law's story, I guessed that if anyone could secure the falcon, it would be he. I knew, too, that no Hansard could!"

"It takes a woman to put two and two together and make five," smiled Sir Anders.

"Still," frowned Sir Olivier, "if you love the boy and would wed him, Jeannette, how can you impoverish him for the sake of a debt I protest you do not owe?"

"Sir, hear me," Frithiof begged. "My uncle bade me say to you, this bird was given to him for his son's ransom; but his son died. Now he gladly gives it to ransom your master's son; and may John of Nevers return alive to gladden his father's heart!"

"There speaks a noble soul," cried Sir Olivier. "Whatever Count John's fate, Duke Philip will repay Sir Lars."

"He wants no payment besides what I myself will give him," began Frithiof. Sir Olivier interrupted.

"Then if the debt is owed to you, to you it shall be paid!"

"You owe me nothing," Frithiof said. "When my uncle bade me home, he offered to make me his heir if I would take over the management of his estates. But I meant to tell him that my father's lands would be enough for me. I wanted to live in Paris, where life is gayer. But since I have won Jeannette, I desire nothing so much as to found a home in Norway for her — and with her. My father and uncle both desire to see me wed and settle here; therefore my uncle sent the falcon with his double blessing."

"God bless you all three, Sir Lars, Frithiof, and

Jeannette," said Sir Olivier. "We will accept this gift you give us as joyfully as men can."

Vahl rode with Frithiof to Sir Lars's home above the city, returning the falcon to its trainer's care since Sir Anders had no mews. Having talked with the man, Vahl recommended to Sir Olivier that the falconer be sent on the next ship to France to deliver the hawk to Philip of Burgundy.

"That is wise," Sir Olivier agreed. "Bajazet must be convinced that we are doing all we can to raise the ransom."

With joyful hearts the knight and squire entered the Hanseatic gaarde a few hours later. They passed beneath the carved wooden figure of the fish-cutter above the arched beam which framed the top of the gate in the wall. Liveried guards led them to the office of the governor.

The alderman sat, richly robed in black, in a magnificent chair of carved oak. His bearing was that of a haughty lord. Penmen, with piles of parchment before them, flanked him on either side, their quills scraping busily. He acknowledged the presence of his visitors with a slight bow.

Sir Olivier stated their business with all courtesy. "We are, sir, the representatives of His Majesty the King of France and His Grace the Duke of Burgundy, sent to you by your ambassador in Paris to take ship to Greenland."

He laid his letter of credit on the table. One

of the scriveners hastily sought out a roll of parchment bearing the seal of the ambassador in Paris, and handed the two to his master to compare.

The Hansard studied them. "Your papers are in order, but we find it inadvisable to send a ship to Greenland this year. I regret that the decision was made so recently that we could not inform you."

"Holy Mary!" gasped Vahl aloud before he could stop himself. Sir Olivier was struck dumb.

"Doubtless," said the Hansard smoothly, "we shall be sending a ship next year. At the moment, we need every vessel for our southern trade. You can understand that it would be poor business for us to risk our money in the northern ice, when the ships can be used with less danger and more profit."

Sir Olivier made an effort to keep his voice calm.

"Unfortunately our business cannot wait until next year. The lives of many worthy knights are at stake, and speed alone can save them."

"The councilors might reverse their decision on one condition," said the Hansard. "Their objection to the voyage is that ship and profits may both be lost, as so many have been — as indeed the vessel we chartered to Greenland last year was lost with all its cargo. If you care to deposit a sum to cover the cost of a ship in case it is wrecked, to lay in the cargo yourself, and to guarantee the Hanse a hundred marks of fine silver in profit, whether or not you return, possibly arrangements may be made."

"But that will take a fortune!" protested Sir
Olivier. "Could we not take ship to Iceland and
find a vessel there to carry us the rest of the way?"

"By royal contract," said the governor stiffly,
"all Greenland trade is confined to this harbor. It
is governed entirely by one family of merchants
within the Hanse, who bought the right to it from
the King of Norway a hundred years ago. I speak
for them. Any Iceland ship voyaging to Greenland
would be confiscated, and its owner heavily fined."

"We have, then, no choice but the terms you
propose?" asked Sir Olivier.

"None," said the Hansard.

"I will give you my decision in the morning,"
said Sir Olivier. He bowed to the official with dis-
dainful hauteur, and led the way to the door.

"That son of Satan!" he exploded the instant
it shut behind them. "A pirate is an honest man
beside him!"

They returned to their host's home angry and
depressed. They found Sir Anders and Frithiof's
father, Sir Nels, deep in conference over the proposed marriage settlement.

"The governor will provide you a ship, never
fear," Sir Anders said. "But you will get it only
on his terms, however hard."

"Captain Gunnar, who commanded the ship
to Greenland two years ago, is now in Bergen. He

might help you decide what to do," suggested Sir Nels. He sent a servant in search of the captain, and Sir Olivier and Vahl waited impatiently for him.

Captain Gunnar was a huge man, well over six feet tall, with a rolling gait acquired from long years on deck. His straight gray hair and long walrus mustaches gleamed like silver against his weatherbeaten face. His eyes were narrowed from long squinting at the sky through wind, sun, rain, and fog; but their frosty gray shone with a lively light. He spoke little French, so Vahl told their story in Norwegian, translating his remarks to Sir Olivier. Once he hesitated, for when he repeated the conversation at the gaarde, the captain burst into a string of curses Vahl had never heard before.

"What does he say?" asked Sir Olivier.

"I do not know myself," said Vahl, laughing. "But I guarantee it contained no word that any priest would approve!"

"Let me take you to Greenland!" roared the captain to Sir Olivier. He seemed to feel unconsciously that if only he yelled loud enough, the knight would understand him. "I will bring you back safely; you need not fear for your deposit on the ship. Part of the hundred mark weight of silver you may lose, but I am a clever trader and I will get what salable goods l can for you to fox those Hansard robbers. The Greenlanders will do their best for us both; they suffer when they are abandoned. I have begged the Hanse these four weeks for a license to sail to Greenland this summer, but they would not let me go. Take their offer, and take me!"

"That I will," said Sir Olivier heartily.

Sir Olivier and Vahl paid another visit to the gaarde next day. Sir Olivier declared that he would accept the governor's terms on two conditions: that he might hire Captain Gunnar's ship, and that his payment of the hundred marks of fine silver to the Hanse would be his full and complete indebtedness for the cargo, whatever its worth. Over these stipulations the governor glowered in silence until Vahl trembled with suspense, but the contract was finally drawn up and signed.

While Captain Gunnar readied his ship, Sir Lars's falconer set off for France to deliver the white hawk. Having failed to pay for the bird otherwise, Sir Olivier took Vahl with him to a fine goldsmith's shop, and there ordered such dower gifts for Jeannette as would have enriched a princess.

It so happened that the Archbishop of Nidaros arrived in Bergen to celebrate a holy day. Sir Olivier and Vahl attended with their friends the High Mass which he celebrated at the cathedral on Sunday. As they left the church, they were astonished to be summoned back by a monk to His Grace's presence.

As they knelt to kiss the Archbishop's ring, they were surprised to see the Italian priest, Father Anselm, standing at his side.

"Father Anselm," the Archbishop explained, "has come to me from the Holy Father in Rome, seeking to learn how the Church stands in all the northern outposts, to confirm its people in their faith, and to collect their tithes. I am told that you have bought the only vessel sailing this year to Greenland where he desires to go. Will you serve Holy Church by permitting the father to be of your company?"

Sir Olivier politely asserted that they would consider the priest's presence a privilege. Vahl knew that no loyal son of the Church could have replied otherwise, but he did hope that the priest would prove more companionable than before. Sir Olivier instructed Father Anselm to be ready to sail in three days. The Archbishop blessed both knight and squire, and promised special prayers for the safety of all their company.

Two nights later, Frithiof brought the Little Lady from Bruges, with his mother's love, as a betrothal gift for her new daughter; and with the queenly manikin beside them, Frithiof and Jeannette were handfasted. Kinsmen and friends, even glum Heinrich among them, drank the betrothal ale. Vahl and Sir Olivier danced the night through at the feast that followed. In the early dawn the whole party walked with them to the wharves through heavy fog and waved good-by to them as they climbed upon the deck of Captain Gunnar's ship.

9

On to Iceland

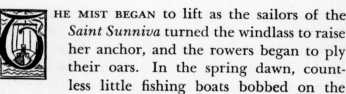HE MIST BEGAN to lift as the sailors of the *Saint Sunniva* turned the windlass to raise her anchor, and the rowers began to ply their oars. In the spring dawn, countless little fishing boats bobbed on the water, skimming out through the islands in the harbor for the day's catch of herring. When he could no longer distinguish the white sail of the last one from the white crests of the waves, Vahl began to take stock of the ship on which he stood.

Its high prow was carved in the likeness of its name-saint, a bright figure with black-painted hair, yellow halo, and flowing blue robes, bravely breasting the swells. The oars were shipped; a stiff east wind filled the heavy, square, blue-and-green striped woolen sail and sent the vessel swiftly through the water. Vahl remembered that Sir Anders and

Sir Nels had bidden him and Sir Olivier give their full trust to Captain Gunnar; otherwise he would have felt certain that so small a ship would sink in the first storm. It was not half as large as the *Man of Ghent* had been. It was fitted with decks only in the bow and stern, with narrow walks along the bulwarks between them. The cargo filled the open hold. Stacked lumber, casks and chests filled every inch and were piled high, covered with weatherbeaten sailcloth to keep out rain and spray.

For calm weather or for entering port, the ship had fourteen long slender oars on each side, seven near the prow and seven near the stern. When he rowed, each of the twenty-eight oarsmen sat upon a bench made out of the sea chest in which he stored his belongings. The crew were all sturdy fellows, mostly young, wearing jackets of oiled and padded leather over knee-length brown woolen tunics. These coats served them as armor against cold, rain, and enemies alike.

Vahl had heard his father tell how, in the old Viking days, warriors on the dragon-headed long ships had hung their shields over the bulwarks, where their metal studdings gleamed like the scales of the monster serpent. The crew of the *Saint Sunniva* did the same, but their leather-covered wooden shields were drab from long weathering. The men wore no weapons — the knives at their belts were only tools — but each man had orders

135

to keep bow and arrow, axe or spear, ready to his hand. Crew and passengers alike slept in the open, each in his leathern sleeping bag. There was room for stretching out, but little more.

After a few hours on the water the ship struck a brief squall. When the company gathered for hot porridge around the iron brazier clamped to the half-deck in the stern, the tossing rendered all three passengers seasick. By the next day Vahl was able to eat again, but during the rest of the voyage to Iceland, Sir Olivier and the priest lived with nothing to stay their stomachs but long draughts of water, and small bits of bread washed down with sips of ale from the captain's cask. They grew white and wan, but their suffering drew them together. Father Anselm produced from his baggage a little folding board marked off and painted in bright squares and a box of chessmen carved of bone. With these the two men passed long hours, while they yearned for the time when they should feel solid land beneath their feet again.

Captain Gunnar watched a few of the matches. For some reason he seemed to regard a good play by Sir Olivier as a personal triumph; the priest's advantages he observed with mere politeness. Captain and crew alike were more cordial to the knight and squire than to Father Anselm.

On the second day the ship passed the Shetland Islands, mere black dots in the south. On the third morning the passengers woke to see land close in the northwest. Rocky cliffs towered out of the sea. Impatiently knight and priest waited for the ship to move closer, until the captain bade Vahl explain that they would not stop.

"Those are the Faroe Islands," he explained. "If a blow came up while we rested in harbor there, it might be weeks before we could get safely out. While we have good weather we had best make what speed we can."

Hearing this, Father Anselm groaned and Sir Olivier drew his belt a notch tighter. But both agreed with the captain's decision.

The ship had no rudder; it was steered by a heavy paddle passing through a grommet of rope on the right side. Captain Gunnar and his first officer, Olaf, acted as steersman, in turn. Vahl liked nothing better than to stand beside them, questioning them about the strange lands toward which they sailed.

"Is it because I have been so long away from the speech of my fathers that your language seems strange to me?" Vahl asked Captain Gunnar one day.

"No, no," said the seaman, stroking his silvery mustaches. "It is because we are Icelanders. We speak Norse, to be sure, but our words have changed somewhat in the five centuries we have lived in our island home. That is the contrary Irish in us."

Vahl was puzzled. "What have the Irish to do with Iceland?"

"They settled half of it," Captain Gunnar explained. "The Vikings settled the other half."

"Was it not always peopled?" asked Vahl, still more perplexed. "I never before heard of any country without folk to dwell in it."

"Iceland was like that," the captain told him. "It had neither man nor snake when the first settlers came — and it has no snakes to this day!"

"Do most of you, then, have Irish blood?" Vahl wanted to know.

"Some more, some less," the captain nodded. "Where did you think this ship got her name, if not from Ireland?"

"I thought Saint Sunniva was a Norwegian saint," Vahl said.

"So she is. Her holy bones are in Bergen Cathedral, and there they work many miracles. But she came from Ireland — all the way from the green isle of Selje in an open boat with neither sail nor rudder nor oars but the will of God. So she belonged to both our parent lands, and we Icelanders took her for our ship's name-saint. She knew the perils of the sea and can intercede with our Lord to spare us from them."

"If Iceland is truly a land of ice, is not the land as perilous as the sea?" Vahl asked.

Captain Gunnar burst into a hearty laugh. "It is not quite that bad," he replied, smiling. "Iceland is icy sometimes, just as Greenland is green — at rare

times and in a few spots. But they should have
changed names long ago. You will see."

The captain had been born in Iceland, though
he had lived in Norway many years. Icelandic trade,
he said, had fallen off as the power of the Hanseatic
League increased. Iceland, like Greenland, was
beginning to suffer from lack of goods which it could
not produce. Fortunately Icelanders still had some
ships of their own. The Greenlanders were not even
that lucky.

"There are not many men left who can chart
a course from Bergen to Greenland," declared the
captain soberly. "If the Hanse ever cuts off trade
completely, the Greenlanders will be as lost to
Europe as if they had drowned in the bottom of
the sea."

Four days after passing the Faroes, the *Saint
Sunniva* cut through endless wastes of water broken
by nothing except the foam of the waves, the gulls
wheeling about the ship, and an occasional ice floe
drifting south. Sometimes the captain altered the
ship's course to steer clear of one of these ice masses,
and a watch was kept to avoid them during the short
northern nights, but apparently they caused neither
captain nor sailors any concern. Only the passengers
felt uneasy about them.

"I draw a breath of relief each morning when
we are still safe," Sir Olivier confessed to the captain.

"If the ship meets no other dangers you need have no fear," Captain Gunnar assured him.

"What else could it meet?" inquired Vahl curiously.

"Pirates," suggested the captain briefly. "The crew is not armed for nothing."

"I prefer a pirate to an ice floe any day," said Sir Olivier. "I can give pirates a warm welcome, but ice is another matter."

They neared Iceland, however, without sighting a single ship, friendly or unfriendly. On the fifth morning, with clouds gathering in the west but a strong following wind to carry them swiftly on, they saw a jagged coastline loom up on their right. A great mountain towered up, snow-covered, into the sky. Gray and forbidding seemed the rocky shore; still it was a welcome sight.

"Is that our port?" asked Sir Olivier hopefully, pointing to the nearest spit of land.

The captain shook his head. "Far from it. We sail the length of the island first. Western Iceland has three great promontories, like three fingers stretching out from a hand. We are bound for Olafsvik on Snaefellsness — Snow Mountain Cape — the central finger."

"Do we pass near Skalholt?" asked Father Anselm.

The captain's jaw dropped. "What do you know of Skalholt?" he asked.

"The learned men of Iceland are held in high repute in Rome," explained the Italian. "Were we not making our journey in haste, there is much I should like to learn from the Bishop at Skalholt."

Captain Gunnar's frosty face warmed toward the priest for the first time.

"Eyrarbakki, the port nearest Skalholt, is on our way westward. With this east wind, we might reach it by dark. Skalholt is a day's ride inland up the White River. I had not thought of it, but you might profit from the trip, Sir Olivier, as well as Father Anselm. The priests of Skalholt are fine falconers and may well possess one of the birds you seek."

"Let us stop there by all means!" ordered the knight. "My skin still sticks to my ribs, but that is more than I can say for anything else!"

Swiftly the ship sped westward with the wind behind it. The sky grew overcast. As the short northern night drew near, the brisk breeze stiffened to a gale and veered toward the south. Straining at the paddle, Captain Gunnar watched the outlines of the nearing rocks with furrowed forehead, but at last he shouted triumphantly above the moaning wind:

"Here is Eyrarbakki!"

Through the growing darkness of storm and night, Vahl saw that they were nearing a low beach. The *Saint Sunniva* anchored among half a dozen bobbing fishing boats as rain began to patter gently down. From the cottages beyond, the fisherfolk came running across the sand. Captain Gunnar shouted a friendly greeting, answered by a dozen voices. Foremost among them, the village priest hallooed to the travellers to follow him quickly. He led the whole crowd scrambling over the rocks to the dry shelter of his little turf-walled church, just as the clouds dropped torrents.

"We have not had such distinguished guests for half a dozen years!" the excited priest told them as they sank panting down on the hard earth floor. "Not since Sir Henry Sinclair, Jarl of the Orkneys, visited Iceland! Are you bound for Skalholt?"

"I must stay with the ship, but these gentlemen wish to go there," said the Captain. "Can horses be had?"

"Every horse in the village is ready for your use if you need it," promised the priest, and the villagers nodded solemn agreement. It was arranged that the priest should guide Father Anselm, knight, and squire, on their journey in the morning. Vahl heard no more of the talk. Leaning against the church wall, he fell dead asleep.

Eyrarbakki in daylight was scarcely even a village — just a few scattered huts clustered about the church. The air was heavy with the smell of fish, spread out after the rain to dry in the sun. Peat, stacked in a big pile, gave off an earthy odor. Cattle

were browsing in some of the distant pastures,
fenced in with lava blocks; nearer, a blacksmith was
shoeing a horse at an outdoor anvil. But few of the
villagers were working; after Mass men and women
all returned to the church with bowls of rich milk,
or plates of fresh fish and boiled greens. Father
Anselm and Sir Olivier smacked their lips over this
simple fare.

The Iceland ponies looked rather moth-eaten,
since they had shed their shaggy winter coats; but
they paced sturdily across the rough lava rocks beside the swift river, through the marshes, hour after
hour, until the travellers reached the ferry. Beyond,
they could see the gabled roofs of Skalholt in a
green valley with a rim of rocky peaks. The guide
pointed out the way to Thingvalla, where in a few
weeks the Icelanders would hold their island assembly and their big market fair, as they had each
summer for hundreds of years. He pointed out,
too, the mountainside far beyond Skalholt where
the greatest of the boiling springs, the Geysir,
spouted its clouds of steam into the air. Vahl would
have liked to see these marvels, but he found Skalholt itself strange enough.

He had thought of it as a city, but in all Iceland
there were no cities — only homesteads, large or
small. Skalholt was the homestead of the Bishop of
the South. Although he owned nothing, the Church
was lord of the whole river valley, and what the

Church owned, the Bishop controlled. Through the three hundred years since Skalholt was established, the bishops had gathered around themselves a great following of priests and lay brothers. At first glance the homestead looked like a town of tiny one-room huts grouped around the tall wooden cathedral. Actually there were not more than a dozen buildings, each with its own outhouses. Because of the difficulty of heating their rooms in winter, the Icelanders built them all on ground level, where each could have its own fireplace. The Bishop's hall, guest house, monastery, school, and farmsteads each had many rooms. Their walls were continuous, but each had its own gabled roof of green turf, so that every large building looked like a cluster of tiny ones.

The ferryman who rowed the travellers across the river conducted them to the guest house. There one of the Bishop's chaplains took Father Anselm and the priest from Eyrarbakki to the Bishop's mansion, while the Father Hospitaller took charge of Sir Olivier and Vahl. Efforts at conversation both in the knight's painful Norse and his white-haired host's still sketchier French resulted in the pleasant discovery that both could speak Latin, so that no interpreter was needed between them.

When he learned his guests' errand, Father Harald shook his head. There was not a single Greenland falcon in Skalholt. But he led the way to the monastery mews, which held several fine Iceland falcons, and suggested that if the pure white birds were not to be had in Greenland, it would be better for knight and squire to take back the darker birds than none at all.

Vahl and Sir Olivier would have liked to try out two of the hawks then and there, but when news of their arrival spread, the Benedictine brothers came crowding about them so eagerly, demanding news of Europe, that they had not the heart to suggest a hunt.

Hospitably the monks insisted that their guests should have a bath. With pride they trooped to the bathhouse, where water from a nearby hot spring was piped into the sunken tub. There, all together, they steamed themselves lobster red luxuriously.

Pleasantly rested and clean, they feasted in the refectory. While they ate tender young rhubarb from the monastery garden, the stout choirmaster stood before them reciting one of the old Icelandic sagas, telling how Snorri the priest, nearly four hundred years before, had begged the chiefs who ruled the country to give up their old Norse gods and worship the White Christ, and how he had won them for his Lord.

With admiration the Hospitaller told the visitors that the chanter was one of the most learned men in all Iceland. Many of the old tales he had at his tongue's end in the very words the bards of old had written.

"Recite to us a story of Greenland," Vahl begged. The choirmaster shook his head.

"The brothers must be about their work. But come you with me; you shall see what our wise men have left us."

He led them to the scriptorium, a quiet room furnished only with sloping stands on which monks laid their parchment when they copied books, and with a great carved wooden cupboard, which the chanter unlocked.

"We have priceless manuscripts here," he said, carefully unrolling a parchment yellowed with age, beautifully lettered in the Latin alphabet and the Norse tongue. "This is one of the oldest telling of Greenland. Iceland had not been settled very long when Icelanders sailed off to look for newer lands. See, this is the saga of Eric the Red, written three hundred years ago, and telling how the Vikings discovered Greenland and Vinland a hundred years before that."

"What is Vinland?" asked Vahl. Sir Olivier, too, looked puzzled.

"It is another land west and south of Greenland," explained the priest.

"I thought Greenland must lie on the very edge of the world," said Vahl, his eyes wide.

The door of the scriptorium quietly opened, and the Bishop of Skalholt led Father Anselm into the room.

"The Holy Father has commissioned this priest his messenger to the far northern outposts," said the Bishop to the chanter, when knight and squire had kissed the Bishop's ring and received his blessing. "He is sent particularly to Greenland and Vinland. But though they belong to his See, the Archbishop of Nidaros could tell him little about Greenland and nothing about Vinland. Can you help him?"

The librarian shook his bald head with its natural tonsure. "I wonder myself if Vinland exists any more," he said. "Certainly it existed once. The old sagas speak of it often — a land of mild weather, rich in wild grapes. The Norsemen found it inhabited by fierce savages, who did their best to drive the settlers away when they tried to build homes along its shore. But it may be that Vinland has vanished as the islands off our coast have been known to do, sinking below the level of the ocean when there is a great earthquake. I have asked many travellers about it, but the tales they have told are all hearsay. When he was here six years ago, Jarl Sinclair of the Orkneys vowed that some day he and his men would voyage to the lands west of Greenland. But whether they did so, I do not know."

"When were the Vinland tithes last paid?" asked Father Anselm.

"Tithes!" The choirmaster's large mouth fell wide open. "If the Vinlanders ever paid tithes, no record of it is here."

"The tithes were paid," said Father Anselm stiffly. He patted his roll of parchment. "I have copies of the records from the Vatican library. But the last payment was in 1325; the Vinlanders have not been heard from since. When he learned of this long silence, it wrung the Holy Father's heart to think how lost his faithful children have been from communion with the Church. Even the tithes from Greenland have not been paid for several years, so I was appointed to visit all the northern outposts and confirm their faith."

"In Greenland your mission is sure to succeed," said the Bishop politely. "But since in all my days I have never met a man who had visited Vinland, I bid you be resigned to God's will if you cannot find a ship sailing there."

"Stay!" cried the librarian suddenly, searching for another parchment. "There is a record of men who visited Markland, at least. Here it is, in the Annals of Iceland."

"Where is Markland?" asked Father Anselm. "I never heard of it."

"It is the wooded country north of Vinland," explained the librarian. "This is the notation: 'In 1347 there came a ship from Greenland less in size than small Icelandic trading vessels. It came into outer Straumfiord. There were seventeen men on board, and they had sailed to Markland, but had afterward been driven hither by storms at sea.'"

148

"What was their story?" demanded the Italian eagerly.

"No more is told," said the monk regretfully.

"Even that gives me hope," said Father Anselm. "That was only fifty years ago, and may well be remembered by living men. The people of Vinland may still exist in their distant country and still cling to the true Faith."

Two days later, when the *Saint Sunniva* had once more put to sea, Vahl seized the first chance to ask Captain Gunnar if he had ever heard of land west of Greenland.

"Heard of it! I have seen it!" cried the captain.

"Have you been there?" queried the dark priest tensely.

The captain shook his head. "No. And I know of no one who has been. But when I made my second voyage to Greenland, my ship was blown six days' sail westward by a contrary gale. When the storm died we saw land to the west — great rocky cliffs."

"Why did you not land?" Vahl asked.

"It was too late in the season; we were afraid of being caught in winter ice. But I have often promised myself to sail there yet."

"Captain Gunnar," begged the priest abruptly, "if the Bishop of Greenland sanctions my going, will you take me to Vinland?"

For an instant the captain hesitated. Then he repeated slowly, "If the Bishop of Greenland bids me take you, I will do it."

"God will bless you as I do!" cried the priest fervently. "I will pray for you with all my heart!" He lifted the cross hanging on a chain about his neck, kissed it, and walked away to a secluded corner of the deck, where he knelt with face uplifted. The captain had a sudden choking fit.

"How dare you, Captain Gunnar, risk the success of our mission by making such a promise?" asked Sir Olivier sternly.

The captain wiped his streaming eyes on his sleeve, and Vahl saw that they were twinkling.

"I risked nothing. The last bishop in Greenland left his post six years ago. But let this tithe-collector find that out for himself."

"You have scant reverence for the representative of Holy Church," scolded the knight, but he also smiled.

The priest spoke to them later, enthusiasm still gleaming from his great brown eyes, of the captain's promise to take him to visit the lost sheep of the Great Shepherd in Vinland. Sir Olivier and Vahl exchanged embarrassed glances, and the knight hastily proposed a game of chess.

IO

The Pirate Ship

T OLAFSVIK, the little fisherman's harbor on the north coast of Snaefellsness, the ship stopped for food and water before leaving Iceland behind. Then winds and ocean currents carried the *Saint Sunniva* quickly westward to Greenland. Many ice floes drifted along the same path, and occasionally a giant iceberg towered out of the water like a great white castle.

At last the travellers saw a snow-capped mountain, blue in the distance, rising out of the mists over the western sea.

"That is the Blue Shirt!" Captain Gunnar pointed out. "It is our first Greenland landmark. Soon we shall see Gunnbjorn's skerries."

"Who was Gunnbjorn?" asked Vahl.

"A Norwegian settler, the first to discover

Greenland, on his way to a new home in western Iceland. Storm-driven, he saw the islands off the coast nearly a hundred years before Red Eric came to explore the country."

"Then our journey must be nearly over," Sir Olivier beamed.

The captain shook his head. "Not yet. We cannot land on this coast. All the interior of Greenland is ice-capped, and on this side the ice sheet covers the land almost everywhere to the very edge of the sea."

"Is it different on the other side?"

"Very different," confirmed the captain. "This is the east side — almost the north. We must sail south until we round the southernmost turning-place. Then it is but a short sail to the Osterbygd, the Eastern Settlement."

The *Saint Sunniva* stayed within sight of the land, but many miles away. The captain explained that inshore from the ocean current with its scattered ice floes, along the headlands and around the island, lay a belt of coast water frozen in winter but full of moving ice in summer; this he must avoid as long as he could. All the travellers could see of the coast was a succession of rocky islands fringing a jagged line of steep, bare headlands.

"We have reached the turning place!" announced the captain cheerily at last. "The end of our journey should be only a few hours away."

His passengers gazed eagerly ahead to see what difference there was between the uninhabited and inhabited coasts. On the farther side, as on the nearer, they could distinguish only desolate wastes of ice and rock.

But as the ship tacked, it was not the land which caught their gaze. In the blue sky to the north, above the icy sea, another sea of ice seemed to hang suspended, upside down. The pinnacles of an enormous iceberg hung inverted, and black against its distant white, a ship sailed steadily upon its mastheads.

"Look, look!" Vahl gasped, while Sir Olivier crossed himself and the priest muttered a hasty prayer.

"It is a mirage," said the captain, but a frown narrowed his eyes to slits as he studied the image, and Olaf whispered to himself, tugging at his beard, "A ship! A ship!"

"Do we actually see a ship where there is no ship?" asked Vahl excitedly.

"We do," said the captain grimly. He raised his voice. "Make your arms ready, men." The deck was instantly quick with movement.

"Surely," said Vahl, laughing, "you do not expect to fight a ship that does not exist?"

The captain eyed him sternly. "This trick of the air and sea does not mean that there is no ship, but only that the ship is not where we see it. It may be far away, it may be near; but somewhere in the northern ice there is a ship where no ship by law should be."

He joined Olaf for a low-voiced consultation, and the sobered Vahl gazed at the mirage again. The black ship moved out of sight, but for half an hour longer the ice field hung in the air like a gray picture on a blue wall. Then a cloud covered the sun, and the image slowly faded. When the sun broke out again, it was gone. Vahl began to polish Sir Olivier's armor.

In midafternoon, Captain Gunnar pointed out a high bleak headland looming on the shore. "Herjolfsness is there. The homestead has a fine harbor at the foot of that mighty rock, and is one of the best trading places in South Greenland. I meant to take you to Ericsfiord, where the chief settlements are, but if there should be a ship in these waters, we had best learn whether it is friend or foe. Shall we land there, Sir Olivier?"

"By all means," said the knight gladly. Olaf pointed the ship inshore, and the sea-weary men rejoiced.

Nearer the land, the pack ice was wedged closer together. The passage of the ship as it edged into the lanes of open water between the ice floes became more and more difficult. Afternoon wore on. Scattered clouds hid the sun. Mist rose, slowing the ship's progress; then the mist became fog, so thick that the steersman could not see to guide the ship, and it drifted helplessly. The offshore breeze stiffened to a high wind, quickening the motion of the tossing ice floes. With the howling of the wind came many another noise. Roaring waves pounded against the rocky shore. Breaking foam hissed wildly. The great ice cakes crashed together, piled one on the other, or broke into huge pieces, with deafening clamor. The ship could only rise and fall with the breaking waves, struggling to keep from being flung against the skerries or the ice. Many were the prayers for safety breathed in the seamen's beards.

Rain fell, and changed to sleet. There was no real night, but the storm brought darkness. The wind howled on. The timbers of the *Saint Sunniva* groaned and creaked, but the stout ship bore itself unharmed through the buffeting of ice and gale.

In the gray light of morning the storm died. The sleet gave way to mist; the mist slowly dissolved into clear sunlit air. Then Vahl saw that the *Saint Sunniva* had been carried once more out into the open sea, with the main current of crashing, moving ice floes between it and the land. Not a landmark of the day before was visible.

"Can we reach Herjolfsness today?" he asked Captain Gunnar, seeing that the captain, too, was studying the coastline.

"We shall not try. We have drifted farther north," said the captain. "Maybe that wind was fortunate for us, for there is Redkammen." He pointed to a snow-clad mountain peak to the east. "Einarsfiord lies below it inside that chain of islands. The chief settlements of East Greenland are all nearby. We shall harbor there."

A stiff breeze still blew off the land, but with furled sail the seamen bent to their oars and advanced into it. Between the ice floes, long open leads offered passage. Through these the *Saint Sunniva* maneuvered, toward a cluster of islands. Rounding one of the outermost skerries into a stretch of open water, the seamen found themselves rowing headlong toward a two-masted ship. With the wind behind it and both sails unfurled, it bore swiftly upon them.

"The mirage ship!" cried Vahl in excitement.

"No mirage!" bellowed the captain. "Stand to your arms!"

The ships were so close that the shouts which went up from the other deck at the sight of the *Saint Sunniva* were clear, and the men on the other ship could be seen seizing their weapons. Big, bearded fellows they were, in heavy leathern garb. Their leader shouted across the space between the ships. The words sounded like neither Norse, French, nor Latin, and no one could make them out, but the brandishing of a sword was no less threatening than their tone. Captain Gunnar shouted back defiantly in his own tongue.

"It is a pirate ship!" muttered Olaf to Vahl, tense beside him. "That is no known flag they fly!"

Attached to the prow of the two-master was a great iron ram. Helped by the wind, the ship raced toward the *Saint Sunniva,* aiming to ram her amidships and finish the battle. But Captain Gunnar shouted quick orders. Olaf and the oarsmen strained every muscle to avoid the blow. The ram struck and glanced off near the prow, swinging the ships almost parallel. It stove in several planks near the waterline, and the captain's quick bark sent three seamen below to repair the damage if they could, while the rest of his crew gathered at the bulwarks, weapons in hand. Out from the enemy ship came a grapnel, locking the *Saint Sunniva* firm in its grip. The pirates tightened the rods of the great iron hook and pulled the ships closer together.

Tensely the men on each side watched the grapnel. The priest stole off to a far corner of the deck and began to tell his beads. The archers bent their bows, and the strings twanged sharply as the arrows sped. The bowmen shot, and shot again. Here and there a howl of pain showed that an arrow found a mark. The gap between the vessels became a dozen yards — ten — six — two. Clearly the battle must be fought out hand to hand, and the archers seized spears and swords. The pirates formed a boarding party in the high forecastle of their ship, ready to leap down on their foes.

"Let us board them from the side!" Sir Olivier cried. Shouting approval, a brave Icelander tried to leap the gap, only to be thrust by waiting sword-arms into the sea. "All together!" shouted Sir Olivier and led the jump, with Vahl and half a score others close at his heels. As they sprang aboard the pirate vessel, the enemy boarding party launched itself upon the deck of the *Saint Sunniva*. Yelling, leaping, thrusting, men on both ships closed in combat with their nearest enemies. Wild shrieks split the air as sword and spear points found their marks. Both decks were soon strewn with wounded men, over whose prostrate bodies the fight continued.

Vahl's place was at Sir Olivier's side, but he could not hold it. The agile knight was everywhere at once; he seemed to find the thickest of the fray by instinct, strike an enemy a disabling blow, and attack another. But Vahl found himself duelling with a short, barrel-chested fellow twice his age and sturdy as an oak. The man beat him back until he could retreat no further except over the deck rail into the sea. Into that icy deathtrap his enemy might have pushed him, had not the pirate suddenly slipped. He recovered too quickly for Vahl to strike him down, but not quick enough to prevent Vahl's safe retreat to the foot of the tiny castle in the stern of the ship. Against him there his assailant again pressed fiercely. He backed Vahl against the cabin door in the wall and set to work with heavy blows to finish him. One of the pirate's comrades, having struck down an opponent, ran to his aid. Together they fell upon the squire.

Vahl glanced wildly about for possible help, but the chance for it seemed slim. Sir Olivier was exchanging powerful blows with the pirate captain some yards away, and the deck between was a melee of flashing swords and twisting bodies. Vahl gathered his strength for a quick blow and succeeded in disabling the second man's wrist. The sword clattered out of his hand to the deck at Vahl's feet, while the man pulled back, screaming with pain. Vahl's first fierce enemy still struck at him, stroke on stroke.

Suddenly Vahl felt the door against which he had wedged himself swing inward. Thrown off balance, he staggered. His foe tried to press home a blow; frantically, Vahl parried it. Then at his feet he felt, rather than saw, the fallen sword snatched up. An ally leaped to his side, a boy younger and smaller than Vahl, and no swordsman. But the lad was fresh while the other two was tired, and his clumsy thrusts took effect. Down went the barrel-chested seaman, sore wounded in the side.

"Quick! Overboard with him!" cried the youngster fiercely. He and Vahl lifted the writhing soldier until they could heave him over the bulwarks.

"Who are you?" panted Vahl to his rescuer.

"A Greenlander. Is that the Bergen ship?" He

did not wait for an answer. "Here, help me! There are others who can fight!"

He ducked back through the door, Vahl behind him. In the dim cabin Vahl could see almost a dozen small forms, with fearful eyes staring at him. His companion motioned to the two nearest — boys of twelve or thirteen, bound with ropes like the rest.

"Cut them free with your dagger!" he begged Vahl. To the others he said, "The rest of you will be safer here. Come, Halvard, Bjorn!" He darted outside, followed by the released prisoners, who dived for weapons fallen on the deck, and squirmed into the fighting.

The pirate captain suddenly struck down Sir Olivier's guard and lunged at his throat. Frenzied, Vahl dashed toward them, reaching his master as the knight stumbled and struck his head hard upon the planks, a dark stain spreading on his breast.

The pirate turned on Vahl with terrible strength and knocked him to his knees at the first blow. But at Vahl's back came the three young warriors from the cabin. Like dogs worrying a bull they surrounded the captain, yelling wildly for help. Before he could even exchange blows with them, two Icelanders rushed into the ring. Against so many foes the captain could no longer stand. Three swords pierced him and he fell.

The Icelanders looked about for new prey, but

the duels nearby were all in their favor, and they gave very leisurely aid in finishing the fighting. Their leader's death disheartened the pirates, and those who fought on were soon overpowered. Vahl knelt beside Sir Olivier, anxious to care for the unconscious man. As he lifted the knight's head into his lap and loosened the fastenings of his hood and jacket, he saw the three young Greenlanders tug at the pirate captain's unresisting body. Lifting it shoulder high, they hurled it into the sea, cheering lustily at the splash. Then they disappeared into the cabin.

Wounded pirates were still struggling in the water with Norse sailors, who clung to their floating shields of leather-covered wood. A few, locked in a death grip or swept under by a wave, sank forever. Several luckier fellows saved themselves by climbing on ice floes, from which they shrieked for help. This the Icelanders hastened to give their comrades, scurrying for ropes which they let down to pull up such wet and wounded as still had strength to cling to them.

Meanwhile, to Vahl's intense relief, Sir Olivier's eyelids fluttered open, and he struggled to sit up, rubbing the back of his head. "A nasty crack," he mourned. "Queer how a man can stave off his enemies and then bash his own brains into oblivion by a stupid fall!"

"I thought the pirate pierced you in the

throat!" Vahl cried. Sir Olivier thrust his hand inside his jacket and felt gingerly about his collarbone. His face crinkled into a smile.

"Truly I believe I owe Dame Louise my life today," he said, drawing out the little reliquary the lady had given him, pierced and broken. "See, this took most of the blow. I got only a bad scratch. Give me a hand to steady me an instant. The dizziness is passing. I can rejoin the battle if need be."

"There is no need. We have won the fight," Vahl said, helping the knight to his feet. He turned to see why Sir Olivier was staring, and beheld the prisoners who had been in the cabin coming toward them with the three boys in the lead. They were all children, thin and frail, their faces disfigured by the stains of weeping.

"Sir," said their leader, the boy Vahl had first seen, "will you take us to your captain?"

"Surely. Follow us," Vahl answered. "We ourselves must report to Captain Gunnar."

"Captain Gunnar? Oh, God be praised, it is he!" cried the children. Waiting no longer for the battle-weary knight and squire who trudged stiffly after them, they ran to the pirate ship's high prow, jumped easily down to the *Saint Sunniva's* deck, and rushed toward the captain with no regard for the grim business he was finishing. Under his direction the last dead and wounded pirates were being thrown overboard, while the small skiff from the pirate ship was lowered to rescue the waterlogged Icelanders.

"Captain Gunnar!" shouted the boy who had come to Vahl's aid, throwing his arms around the captain's neck with such strength that the man almost reeled. "Captain Gunnar!"

"Baard Asbrandsson! How did you come here?" cried he. If he said more, his words were smothered by screams of joy as the other children clutched at him and clung to him.

"The pirates kidnapped us for slaves while we were gathering birds' eggs yesterday along the shore cliffs," Baard explained when he could be heard. "Take us home, Captain Gunnar!"

"Stand off or I will take you nowhere!" roared the captain with pretended harshness.

"You are wounded!" gasped Gunhilda, the oldest girl, as the crowd of children fell back. The old man's left arm hung limp.

"It is nothing." But the captain winced as Olaf and Sir Olivier stepped quickly forward to examine the hurt. "I would have been dead but for Father Anselm. He can fight as well as pray!"

Vahl stared at the priest. He stood quietly by the mast, his left hand fingering the cross which hung from his neck. But his right sleeve had been rolled up, and the arm showed muscular, its hand still clenched about the hilt of a sword.

"Could I do less for the friend who has promised to take me to Vinland?" Father Anselm answered.

"Vinland!" exclaimed young Baard, his eyes bulging. Captain Gunnar's face, red from exertion, turned still redder. He gulped.

"We will do well to get safe ashore!" shouted a sailor. "That hole in the *Saint Sunniva's* side is still letting in water!"

"Sir!" shouted the boy Baard, "I know how to reach Einarsfiord the quickest way! Let me guide you in!"

"Every man to the oars!" shouted the captain. "Let the grapnel hold the ships together! The pirate boat would save us if the *Saint Sunniva* sank, but I mean to keep them both!"

With all his skill learned in camp and field, Sir Olivier quickly dressed the captain's wounded arm, while Olaf took the helm. Under Baard's direction, the boats slid cautiously between the islands and came at last with exhausted crews into the open waters of a wide fiord. As the ships anchored in the shallow water, men appeared running on the high rocks above, shouting a greeting.

II

Falcon Nest

ROM THE FATHER of Baard, the voyagers learned how the children had been taken by the pirates. Asbrand and his men had come seaward down the fiord the day before for a walrus hunt. While their children scoured the cliffs along the shore for birds' eggs, the men had rowed beyond the end of the bay. One of the hunters had seen the pirate ship, but too late to call the others back. Returning with their kill, the men had found the children gone, and despaired of seeing them again.

Now with shouts of joy and fervent embraces, they gathered on the rocky meadow girdling the harbor, hastening to help the Icelanders. With the *Saint Sunniva* safely beached, the pirate ship moored, and the wounded men cared for, all the Greenlanders crowded around to hear the travellers' errand.

"Eight Greenland falcons!" mused Asbrand, resting his chin on his hand. "That is a large order. The birds are common enough, but they nest on inaccessible cliffs, and great craft is required to capture them."

"Our whole cargo is payment for them," said Sir Olivier.

"Do not mention payment!" protested Asbrand. "Have you not brought back our children, who are worth more to us than all the other wealth of Greenland? If we have anything you covet, it is yours for the asking."

"Your lads gave as well as received aid in the battle." Sir Olivier smiled at Baard. "For any falcons your people secure us, we must pay. Otherwise my lord Philip will consider that his representatives have dishonored him."

Asbrand bowed as Vahl relayed this speech, and replied with a manner as knightly as the courtier's, "I lost my son only for a day, yet I know the feelings of a father whose son is kept from him for many weary months. If the falcons can be caught, my people and I will catch them."

Sir Olivier began to express his thanks, but Asbrand paid no heed. A Greenlander had touched his arm, muttering tensely. Asbrand, who had before shown only sincere concern for his guests' errand, suddenly became deadly serious. His lean, muscular right hand gripped Sir Olivier's shoulder.

"I said we would take no payment from you, and I meant it from my heart. Yet there is a payment you could make to us which we would take gladly. Aye! we would beg you for it on our knees."

Asbrand's voice began to tremble. Wondering, Sir Olivier bade Vahl have him name it; and steadying his voice, Asbrand spoke again. "Lend us one of your ships for a voyage to the Western Settlement!"

"The Western Settlement —" Vahl echoed, puzzled. Then he thought he understood. "Oh, you mean Vinland!" he cried eagerly.

"No, no!" Asbrand shook his head. "Vinland lies west and south across the sea. The Western Settlement is in Greenland, far up the coast, beyond valleys choked with ice."

"I had almost forgotten it ever existed," said Captain Gunnar. "No ship has sailed there in my days at sea. The Hanse forbade it after the people there were supposed to have been destroyed by Skraellings."

"Well do I know it," answered Asbrand grimly. "We have not heard from our kinsmen there for fifty years. Yet for all we know, they may still survive. It is the same with our kinsfolk in Vinland; we cannot learn how they fare, because we have no seaworthy ship."

"Could we find falcons in the Western Settlement?" asked Vahl.

"They should be as common there as here," Asbrand declared.

"Let us strike a bargain," suggested Sir Olivier. "If the *Saint Sunniva* can be made seaworthy again, we shall have two ships, and we need but one. We will loan you the pirate vessel for a voyage to the Western Settlement, and to Vinland if time allows. Meanwhile bid your men capture what falcons they can. It may be that we must take the pirate ship for our voyage home, but if we can secure the eight birds we seek and if the *Saint Sunniva* is once more fit for use, we will sail in her back to Bergen, leaving behind us the pirate ship in payment."

"Well and good, but while I am here, both ships stay under my command!" cried Captain Gunnar. "If a ship sails, I sail with it! No such chance to see the world is going to pass me by, while I can laugh at the Hanse from a ship which does not sail under their restrictions!"

"On so great a matter I dare not speak alone," said Asbrand, locking his hands together to keep them from shaking with excitement. "Be at home with us here in Einarsfiord until I can call the men of the Osterbygd to a Thing to hear what you propose. They shall answer you."

Greenlanders in their little skiffs, Icelanders in the pirate ship — the whole party rowed for six hours up the fiord. Vahl soon forgot his aching muscles in the warm, bright sunshine. It was strange to see no trees anywhere; but Greenland was green indeed, with scrubby thickets of willow and juniper, and long grassy meadows where little herds of cattle, sheep, and goats munched contentedly among brilliant flowers. Far inland, beyond the head of the wide sunken river valley, towered the peak of Redkammen. The mountain was the center of a horseshoe of hills which encircled the valleys of Einarsfiord. Below Redkammen the fiord divided, one branch turning south to Gardar, the other north to Krakortok, or White Rocks.

Near this bend, a cluster of small boats waited for the travellers. One of Asbrand's men had paddled through the night to carry news of their coming. Father Anselm was given reverent welcome by a monk and two lay brothers from Gardar. The lay brothers could talk to him only by smiles and signs, but the monk proudly managed a few words in rusty Latin. The priest set off with them for their monastery, eager to begin his work at once. Sir Olivier had expected to take quarters in the monastery for himself and Vahl also, but Asbrand offered them hospitality so urgently that they could not refuse. Bidding farewell to Captain Gunnar and the crew, who remained with the ship at anchor, they set out in Asbrand's skiff, with their host and his children, Baard and Gunhilda.

Krakortok was built on sloping meadows on the north side of the fiord, walled on the inland side by tremendous white cliffs. Asbrand's home stood above and beyond the cluster of little stone huts where his retainers lived. Houses and barns alike were roofed with turf, now green with grass and bright with flowers. Vahl noticed that some families had removed pieces of their roofs and were flooding their little homes with light. Baard explained that the stone interiors were often damp, and that nothing dried them so quickly as bright sunshine.

Even Asbrand's home, by farm standards in the warmer world, was small. Vahl counted four tiny gables, and one longer roof, so that he could easily guess his friends' house had four rooms besides its hall. Like the retainers', it was stone, the chinks filled in with blue clay or stuffed with sod. The only thing to show that Asbrand, the chief man of White Rocks, lived any better than his followers was that his house had a pane of clear glass in the narrow window of each room, while the poorer folk had windowpanes of walrus gut.

"Be welcome beneath this roof," said Gunhilda at the door. "I must leave you now to see that food is prepared."

"My daughter is mistress of the homestead," Asbrand explained. "Her mother rests in holy ground." He opened the weatherbeaten plank door, led the way through a low vestibule with a stone threshold, and motioned his guests into the hall.

Across the far end of the room stretched a high

stone platform, in two levels. The lower step was simply a very wide stone bench, like the two built down the adjoining sides of the room. The upper step was even wider. Low benches and high seat alike were covered with thick furs and at either end of the dais were piled pallets of eider duck feathers and heaps of fur rugs. These were kept ready for bedmaking, since the household seats were also the household beds.

A warping frame and a loom threaded with coarse wool made up all the furniture except for the long stone fireplace in the center of the beaten earth floor, with a smoke vent above it in the roof. The hearth was swept clean of fuel and fire. In that fuel-starved country, as Vahl found later, heat and light both came only from the small double stone lamp which hung suspended by an iron rod from a rafter. The small upper basin held seal-oil; the lower and larger caught the drippings.

Vahl, after a quick glance around, with his heart sinking at the poverty of the place, asked Baard, "Could we see the mews?"

The mews was only a deserted stone shed. It had a few perching blocks, crudely shaped of stone, and some old leather hoods and leashes, but little else.

"Where are your falcons?" asked Vahl in astonishment.

"We have none," Baard told him.

"With the finest hunting birds in the world," Vahl cried, "you do not use them?"

"Not any more," Baard explained. "In the time it takes a falcon to strike down one sea bird, we can snare a dozen. But we catch the hawks to sell when we can."

"How do you carry the eyases?" asked Vahl, looking around in dismay. Plainly he must work hard at fashioning equipment. There was no sign of the woven reed hampers he had expected to see.

"In a leather bag," said Baard. "We have plenty in the storehouse."

"Let us get one and start hunting this afternoon," Vahl suggested.

"If you wish," agreed Baard. "But why carry it today? The season is hardly late enough to find eggs hatched, much less eyases grown to a size that will live in captivity. All we can hope for today is to find a nesting place."

"Then we cannot hope to finish our business here until several weeks pass!" exclaimed Sir Olivier.

"No, sir, truly," Baard answered. "It was only for that reason that my father dared to propose your loaning him a ship."

That night Sir Olivier spoke to Vahl about the visit to the Western Settlement.

"If the falcons are to be found there, one of us should go on that voyage."

"I thought we would both go," said Vahl.

Sir Olivier shook his head. "We have learned for a certainty there are falcons here. One of us should stay. Which shall it be?"

"It is my place," said Vahl, hiding his disappointment because he could see the good sense in the knight's words. "You shall take with you what equipment there is, and what I can make before you go. Then I can refurnish the mews here as need arises."

"Good!" exclaimed the knight. "I am glad you do not begrudge me the journey."

For some days, while Asbrand sent retainers far and wide to call homesteaders to the Thing, Baard and Gunhilda roamed the meadows of Einarsfiord with their guests, looking for falcons. They saw several, but were never able to track them to their nests. Then Asbrand decided to take Baard, knight, and squire, on a hunting trip up Icyfiord. This was the most northern valley of the Eastern Settlement, where a tongue of the inland glacier thrust into the water at the head of the fiord. The travellers were fascinated by this river of ice, which stretched back between the hills until it joined the great white sea of ice above.

Asbrand and Baard beached their boat in a sheltered inlet and made camp at a deserted old stone farmhouse. Men and boys separated, each armed with bow and arrows. The men explored the valley cliffs along the headlands while the boys stalked quarry toward the glacier. They feasted on hare and wild duck during two days of wandering, watching for homing falcons. They saw some of the hawks, but never flying twice in the same direction, at least on their side of the fiord. One pair, however, seemed to haunt a cliff on the other side, so the hunters decided to cross.

"Could we walk over the glacier?" asked Vahl.

"If you are surefooted," agreed Asbrand.

They walked up the valley through the low willow, birch, and juniper tangles; over carpets of buttercups and dandelions, bluebells, and clumps of red and yellow saxifrage; through boggy places where cotton grass waved its white tufts; among pinks, mustards, and roses; and through beds of white and yellow poppies on the dryer slopes, to the front of the glacier.

It rose straight out of the water for about two hundred feet, but it was not the smooth, solid wall it appeared from far away. Surface water, melted from the ice by the sun, cascaded down the face. Behind this, the cliff was a fantastic façade which reminded Vahl of the great town hall of Bruges, so elaborately carved did the ice appear with its niches and pillars. But the design changed continually, for bits of ice and snow kept crumbling away and splashing into the river below. At intervals a sharp crack sounded, and a larger chunk of ice would be torn loose. For awhile it would bob like a big cork in the water, then float away with the other bergy bits.

Partly to avoid danger from the breaking off of such ice fragments at the tip of the glacier and partly to find an easy slope along its side, men and boys walked some distance up the valley to a point where the ice river narrowed between two rocky cliffs. The edges of the glacier did not cling solidly to the rocks, but shrank away, leaving a narrow gorge. The sloping side of the glacier was not hard to climb there, for embedded stones and dirt gave foothold.

Vahl expected the top of the glacier to be smooth, but it was cracked every few score yards by a great crevasse. These openings ran upriver and inward, so irregularly that they often crossed. The ice ridges separating them were slippery, and the party kept careful watch lest a misstep should send one of them skidding helplessly into a deep canyon. Many times they were forced to retrace their steps, when two crevasses came together, leaving a gap too wide to be leaped.

Toward the middle of the glacier the ice was fairly smooth. Little streams of water flowed over the surface toward the sea until they reached some crack, down which they tumbled to swell the underground torrent which rumbled along below the ice with a sound like distant thunder.

On the other side the crevasses were larger, and the hunters made slow progress. Sometimes they had to crawl on hands and knees or stretch out flat and writhe forward to keep from slipping into a dangerous crack. In the summer sun, with ice melting everywhere, such parts of their bodies as they could keep dry were comfortable enough, but these were small. The four were soon wet and shivering.

They had almost reached the far shore when, working their way between two crevasses, they came out upon a point of ice beyond which the openings met. To jump across was impossible: the space was too wide. Moreover, the farther ice-shelf was higher than the near and offered no handhold. But Baard lagged behind the others as they turned to take a long way around. Suddenly he shouted:

"Here is a way across!"

They saw the boy sit down and slide out of sight. His distressed father, hurrying back, found him astride a narrow natural bridge of ice, pulling himself forward by his bare hands.

"Come back, Baard!" Asbrand cried. "That bit of ice may fall under your weight!"

"No, no, it is perfectly safe!" protested Baard, and bounced his body to prove it. Vahl shut his eyes, expecting to see the thin ice crack and drop the boy to his death. But the ice held rigid. Even if Baard had wanted to, he would have had a hard time coming back. The curve in which the ice-bridge had melted made it harder to push back than to pull forward.

176

When Baard had crossed successfully, Asbrand tested the ice-bridge as well as he could, and decided to risk following Baard's example. He and Sir Olivier pulled themselves safely over. Vahl started after them. Half way, he thought disgustedly that nervousness must be making him dizzy as he looked at the icy river below him; then he realized that the ice-bridge had begun to slip as Asbrand had feared.

"Help me!" he cried.

They heard the ice-bridge begin to crack. Asbrand instantly flung himself flat on the ice and stretched out his hands to meet Vahl's. In a moment Sir Olivier was flat beside Asbrand, his leather belt off and in his hand.

"Go easy!" Asbrand breathed. "Pull gently!"

"Take hold of my belt!" Sir Olivier begged, dangling it down as far as he dared. Vahl touched it, inched along until he could get a good grip, and then felt himself pulled steadily up the icy incline. Two strong hands seized him and pulled him flat on his face in the slush. Behind him a sharp crack sounded. The ice-bridge still held its shape, but the sun glinted on a break from top to bottom.

"I'll be glad to get back to solid ground!" smiled Vahl shakily.

Fortunately the remaining crevasses were narrow, and the quartet soon reached the other side. Clinging to embedded rocks which kept them from slipping far, they made a safe descent.

The gorge on the east was much rougher than on the west and showed more signs of the tremendous power of the ice as it moved forward. Asbrand said this was because the slope of the hills was steeper and resisted its free flow more. Great ridges of rock had been piled up by the glacier, which bowled along huge stones the size of a Greenland house. The rocks below the ice must have been uneven, for as the group walked through the gorge toward the head of the glacier, they passed wide clefts opening up from the bottom and closing over, high up, like the arches of a great cathedral.

Baard persuaded Vahl to stand with him under one of the arches; but water dripped on their heads, and the roar of the underground river was deafening. When a sharp crack like caged lightning sounded over their heads, they stumbled speedily out into the gorge again.

To warm their drenched, cold bodies, they strode briskly seaward along the base of the valley cliffs. Soon they saw one of the falcons above the meadows and marked the precipice upon whose ledges it disappeared and from which it soon flew away.

Like all the heights above the valley, the one where the falcons nested was steep, but it was not inaccessible. The Greenlanders, used to finding toe- and handholds on slippery surfaces, soon worked their way up, and shouted down that a nest was

178

there. Sir Olivier and Vahl then clambered up also and saw a falcon's nest for the first time: a mass of woody brush in which lay two brownish-white eggs. After one glimpse they all climbed quickly down, not wishing the parent birds to take fright and desert the nest.

"Our trip has been well worth while," declared Sir Olivier. "Now we know where to come for two eyases for John of Nevers' ransom!"

"Look!" cried Baard, pointing to the front of the glacier. "The ice is moving!"

Vahl could see nothing. But peals of thunder rumbled out of the ice, followed by a mighty crash. Then he noticed that the sculptured face was slowly rising out of the water. New arches and new caves pushed up.

"The glacier is going to calve," said Asbrand, watching intently.

A deep, dull rumble filled the air again, ending in a loud peal which echoed among the cliffs. The glacier front rose faster. Two or three large fragments broke off, sending spray flying high.

"Let us go down to the shore and watch it," suggested Sir Olivier. Without waiting for any reply, he ran blithely toward the water's edge.

"Come back!" shouted Asbrand. "Come back!" screamed Baard.

A fearful crash seemed to come from the very point of the ice tongue. The pillars and arches, high in the air, sank fast beneath the water, crumbling as they sank. Then the spray cast up by the splashing fragments hid the ice in foam and mist. Other spires and pinnacles toppled. The roar of sound as they fell grew and grew until it filled the valley. Vahl felt as if his eardrums would burst.

Sir Olivier rushed back up the slope toward his companions, but not quickly enough. Through the spray cast up by the breaking ice rose a mighty wave, swelling outward and curling up the rocky shores like a roaring monster.

"Hold fast to a rock!" shouted Asbrand with all his strength, his words faint through the noise of the water. The three on high ground clung tight to boulders while the wave rushed on them, but the knight was swept from his feet and rolled cruelly down the rough rocks. He got to his knees and seized hold of a huge stone just as a second swell knocked him prostrate once more. Four waves rushed up the hillside, but each with lessened force. Vahl and his companions rose to their feet, dripping but unharmed. Sir Olivier lay unconscious, still clinging to his rocky anchor. In the fiord floated a huge iceberg, half a mile across, on its way to the sea.

They ran down to the knight, calling his name, but he did not answer. Vahl held his breath until he felt the man's pulse beat faintly under his fingers. At last Sir Olivier's eyelids fluttered, and his sense returned. He tried to sit up and fell back with a groan. When the two boys supported him so that he could rise, he did so, though his face whitened. But his leg was broken, and he could not stand.

"We can never get him to shelter except by boat," Asbrand muttered. "I will get it." Without an instant's hesitation, he strode up the valley.

"If only the boat is still there!" Vahl thought, and saw the same worry in Baard's face. But they busied themselves rubbing the knight's cold hands. Then Baard cut branches for splints, while Vahl tore strips from his shirt to bind them on.

All three rejoiced when they saw Asbrand rowing toward them. The boys made a stretcher of their jackets on the oars to carry Sir Olivier. Then Vahl held him in his arms, while the others rowed. The water was still choppy. From time to time they heard the glacier rumble and crack again, but Asbrand risked a straight crossing. Small layers of ice, flaking off, tossed the boat, but did no harm.

At the deserted farmhouse, fire and food soon revived them all. Asbrand skillfully rebound the broken leg, and sent the boys to gather soft dry branches on which the injured man could lie. When they returned, Sir Olivier said cheerfully to Vahl:

"At least I have helped to find one falcon's nest in Greenland. Now if it be so that I can climb after no others, I shall turn falconer and tend the mews, while you, my boy, make the voyage to the Western Settlement."

12

Beyond The Uninhabited Coast

VEN AFTER Sir Olivier had been brought
safely back to White Rocks, it was still
some days before the homesteaders of the
Eastern Settlement could gather for the
Thing. Though the knight had given up
the voyage to the Western Settlement because of his
injury, he was determined to go to the Assembly
even if he had to be carried.

Asbrand put all his serving folk at the knight's
call, but Gunhilda insisted on being his nurse. She
waited upon him from morning till night with clever
hands and cheerful face. When no one but Vahl
was by, she taught Sir Olivier the Greenland tongue
and learned French from him. Vahl thought she was
astonishingly quick and bright. He was delighted
to spend his time with her and the invalid, making
falcon gear from bits of old soft leather. He wanted

a good supply for the voyage, and more to leave behind for use in Asbrand's mews.

Baard stayed with them when he could, and he and his sister shortened many hours telling tales of their kinsman Einar, who had come with Eric the Red from Iceland in the year 986, and for whom Einarsfiord was named. They told how Eric's followers had settled both the Eastern and the Western Settlements in Greenland, and lived comfortably in them for 250 years until trade with Iceland and Norway dwindled and was at last forbidden. Finally Osterbygd and Vesterbygd were cut off from each other for lack of seagoing ships. In 1343, after years of worry, the Eastern Settlement sent its biggest fishing boat to the Western Settlement. It found only Skraellings there, and the timid leader retreated without learning the fate of the homesteaders. The Osterbygd had never had another ship to send, though many people felt sure their kinsmen might still survive.

Baard and Gunhilda told, too, how Leif, Eric's son, in the year 1000, found a warm and pleasant country south and west across the sea from Greenland, which he called Vinland because of its plentiful wild grapes. They told how Leif, sailing homeward from Vinland, found another country which he called Markland, which means Woodland, because the trees there crowded down to the very shores of the sea. And still another land Leif found, north and east of Markland, which he called Helluland, or Flagstoneland, because there tier on tier of barren rocks stretched inland from the sea.

They told how Leif's brother Thorstein and his half-sister Freydis and Thorfinn Karlsefni of Iceland had tried to establish homes in Vinland, but had been driven out by the wild native Skraellings. They told how other folk, too, had gone to live in Vinland, or to bring timber from Markland, some with good luck and some with bad, and more of whom nothing had afterward been known.

"I shall have the best of our travels after all," Sir Olivier teased Vahl as he listened to these stories. "When you have hunted falcons in the Western Settlement, I shall go to hunt them in Vinland."

Some of their tales the sister and brother sang in verse. Baard had a pleasant voice, but Vahl thought Gunhilda's the sweetest he had ever heard. Secretly he wondered if it reminded Sir Olivier of his lost wife; he could understand how the knight had fallen in love with such an angel's voice. In any case the knight never tired of hearing the lays, and he sent to the ship for his lute, which he taught Gunhilda to play. With her quick ear and nimble fingers she could soon make melodies. She was enchanted for in all Greenland there was no longer a musical instrument.

"Even when we dance, our only music is a song," she said wistfully.

"Not while I am here!" declared Sir Olivier. When he learned that the Thing would end with a dance, nothing contented him until he could play the tunes. When he practiced them, Gunhilda, singing merrily, put Vahl through the steps until both dropped down exhausted and laughing on the stone benches, their hands clasped together.

At last came the day for the assembly. In the early morning Sir Olivier was lifted on a stretcher and borne by Asbrand's men to the boat which was to take him and the young people to Gardar. In Eric's day the Thing had met at his estate on Ericsfiord. But from the time that Greenland's first bishop came, in 1126, the Thing was held in the close of the cathedral which was built for him on the southern fork of Einarsfiord. There the homesteaders had arrived, family by family, and had set up their skin tents in the meadows.

Until the day of the meeting neither Vahl nor Sir Olivier had visited Gardar. Between the Bishop's homestead on one side and the monastery on the other, stood the Cathedral of St. Nicholas, shaped like a cross. It was the pride of the people because its windows had once been all of stained glass, though in the course of years two had been filled with transparent panes.

Mass was sung by Father Anselm in a voice so magnificent that it reached out of the packed little cathedral to the farthest worshipper kneeling on the ground outside. Then the Greenlanders gathered in orderly array out of doors. The chief man of Brattahlid, a descendant of Eric, presided; but he was a young lad and deferred in all things to the judgment of the older chiefs.

The meeting was strange to Vahl and Sir Olivier, for they had never known any land in Europe where lords and peasants gathered to decide together how they should be ruled. In Greenland one man had as good right as another to speak his mind, whether he was herdsman, hunter, or priest. Matters were decided by voting.

Father Anselm and Captain Gunnar joined Sir Olivier to listen to the proceedings. What knight and priest could not understand, Vahl translated for them. He was too eager to hear what the Greenlanders would say to notice how the priest smiled at Asbrand's first mention of the proposed visit to the Western Settlement. He did not see how the smile died, and the priest's black brows drew together over angry eyes.

Vahl felt his breath come quick as the Greenlanders began to shout approval. One and all they showed their hands when Asbrand called for falcon-catchers and for crew. Plainly, if the visitors' mission failed, it would not be for want of aid.

Vahl had no time to rejoice over this with Sir Olivier. He felt a hand grip his arm, and turned to face the tense priest.

"The captain, then, knew that no bishop lives in Greenland now? He knew that even if a bishop had been here, he was forbidden to take his ship on such an errand as he promised me?"

Startled and dismayed, Vahl slowly nodded. Father Anselm clenched his hands and demanded, "Why did he deceive me? Ask him why!"

Timidly Vahl approached the captain, who was thumping Sir Olivier's shoulder in congratulation, and translated the question.

"Tell the titheman to look about him," said Captain Gunnar, staring the angry Italian straight in the eyes. "He will understand."

The priest's black brows knit more tightly, but his glance followed the captain's motioning hand and lingered on the throng. No one could miss the captain's meaning. In all that crowd, which held the greatest men of Greenland, not one but was as meanly dressed as a French peasant. Their long, homespun woolen tunics and hoods were threadbare and patched, one and all. Nor were the people, Vahl thought, poorer in clothing than in the rest of their lives. If hard work in their harsh climate brought them shelter and food, they considered themselves fortunate.

"Whatever may have been between us," declared the captain, drawing back the priest's gaze by the steadiness of his own, "you saved my life, and I brought the ship safely into port which alone can take you where you wish to go. I am glad my promise to you will be kept."

The priest turned without a word, and stalked away.

"Yet why should the Holy Church of our merciful Redeemer send that sheepshearer here?" growled Captain Gunnar to Vahl under his breath. "These poor stragglers of God's faithful flock need their thin wool!"

The pirate ship, new-christened the *Good Shepherd,* was ready for the voyage to the Western Settlement as soon as the Greenland crew was chosen. It was to sail at dawn on the third day after the Thing ended, and boats from all the homesteads gathered to bid its men good-by. Foremost rowed the monastery boat from Gardar, bringing Father Anselm. He mounted the deck with his gear and took his place beside Vahl, with the calm air of a rightful passenger.

Sir Olivier spoke gravely to Vahl before they parted. "I have but jested about Vinland. If you think you can catch falcons at the Western Settlement, stay a few days. Otherwise, return here swiftly. The Greenlanders believe they can soon find all the birds we need; and if they do, we should be off for home at once. I hope they can make the Vinland voyage, but it is not for us."

Under Captain Gunnar's command, with Asbrand as steersman and Baard among the men at the oars, the *Good Shepherd* began its trip up the uninhabited coast beyond Icyfiord. Though men could not live in the ice-filled valleys, seals, walrus, and sea birds abounded on the beaches. Ice bears, too, appeared several times. The sailors' hands itched for their hunting weapons, but they rowed on steadily. They gloried in their work, for none of them had ever sailed before in a vessel stout enough to venture freely into open ocean.

On the evening of the second day, the captain bade the seamen anchor the ship on the edge of a giant iceberg. There was no real darkness, but twilight and fog made him fear that they might pass, unseeing, the valleys of the Western Settlement.

Vahl slept heavily, but woke in the clear blue dawn to see Asbrand standing at the bulwarks. The boy joined him quietly.

"Do you see anything, sir?"

Asbrand smiled. "Only the vision of folk lost for fifty years."

"I dreamed of the iceberg," Vahl said, gazing at the great white field rising out of the blackness of the water. "But it was a monster in a nightmare."

"Monster it is, when a storm tosses the sea," Asbrand agreed. "But in weather like this, it is sometimes friendly as a farm, stocked with beasts for food and watered by the melting snow."

"Could I walk on it while the others sleep?" Vahl asked.

"By all means," said Asbrand. "Take Baard with you, and bring back some fresh water."

Baard jumped up, wide awake, when Vahl whispered his proposal. He picked up a spear, motioned Vahl to buckle on his sword, and each with a leather bucket they dropped over the bulwarks.

"Why the armor?" Vahl wanted to know.

"We may be near Skraelling country," Baard explained.

Where the ship was anchored, the ice of the berg came down almost to the waterline, like a beach, for perhaps a quarter of a mile. But hillocks and valleys along the low shore became pinnacles and towers toward the far edge, where a white wall of ice reared several hundred feet into the air.

The boys wandered along until they came to a wide depression where the melting snow had formed a lake. The morning light was growing, so they filled their buckets and chose what they thought was a straight path to the ship. As they came quietly around a sheltering ice hummock, Baard, in the lead, stopped and motioned Vahl back.

"There's a seal asleep! I'm going to kill it for meat!"

Setting down his bucket, he went flat on the ice, and wriggled silently forward. The seal slept on. Vahl lay down and wriggled after Baard.

The seal suddenly raised its head, wide awake. Baard stilled every muscle. The creature shut its eyes and slept again. Baard crept closer.

Around the other side of the hummock stole another silent hunter. A huge yellow-white ice bear had seen the seal too. Unconscious of him, Baard, now on his feet, lifted his spear for a killing stroke.

"Look out!" shrieked Vahl. Baard stood paralyzed. The startled seal jerked madly toward the sea. The bear, bounding forward, caught sight of the boy and the boy of him. Motionless they stared a second; then each fled to his own side of the hummock.

"What are you running for?" Vahl cried, doubled up with laughter as Baard dashed past him. "That bear was so scared he's on the other side of the iceberg by now!"

"Maybe!" gasped Baard, not slacking his pace. Vahl had to sprint to catch up with him.

"I can't carry water at this pace!" he protested.

"Drop the buckets!" Baard snapped. "Look behind you!"

The bear had emerged from behind a nearer hummock. With its long snaky neck outstretched, it padded along, sniffing at the boys' track. Swift as they ran, the beast loped easily behind. Vahl glanced to see if it was gaining, stumbled, and fell sprawling. His cap fell off his head and slid over the ice. Baard jerked him to his feet.

"Hurry! Faster!"

The bear was only a few score yards away. But the moving cap caught its eye; it turned to paw and smell. The boys raced on. The bear, lumbering after them, made no sound, but his great hairy feet shortened the distance between.

"Lord, save us!" gasped Baard. He tore the cloak off his shoulders and threw it backward across the ice. The curious bear paused again, his great jaws snapping at the cloth. No taste of the fresh meat he smelled satisfied him; he growled, thrust the object aside with a tearing claw, and bounded forward, as the boys rounded the last ice-ridge that hid them from the ship.

"Help!"

Heads popped up over the bulwarks. But the bear was so close Vahl imagined he felt its hot breath. He flung his own cloak behind him; it billowed over the beast's head. In the second before the animal shook it off, Baard turned and thrust his spear deep in its neck; then dodged to one side. Roaring, the wounded animal turned on him. Vahl was too distant to strike; with all his strength he hurled his sword like a harpoon. It scarcely scratched the bear's flank, but attacked on two sides, the beast wavered between his enemies. Men tumbled over the ship's side, spears in hand, and ran shouting toward the bear. He charged, but an arrow quivered in his shoulder, another in his neck. He turned to retreat too late. A ring of spears surrounded him.

When the animal's heavy, eight-foot body had been lifted to the deck by ropes, and the men had skinned it, Vahl gazed longingly at the thick, oily fur.

"Could I buy it?" he asked. "It would be quite a souvenir of a peaceful morning walk."

"It is yours already," Baard told him. "The skin always goes to him who sights the bear first, and the choice of the meat to him who first wounds it. That is the custom."

Vahl's protests fell on deaf ears. "It is the custom," settled every argument. While the ship turned in toward the rocky headlands of a great green valley like those in the Osterbygd, skilled men began to dress the skin for him.

"But the next time you laugh at anyone running from a bear," said Baard privately in his ear, "may the beast make sausage-meat of you!"

The *Good Shepherd* was rowed far up the fiord, the men watching for signs of life. Clear eyes soon saw a stone farmhouse, but it had no roof. Another farm, and then a third, looked equally lifeless, but the oarsmen pressed forward to the head of the fiord, where the stone buildings of a village spread over the valley. From the gray church above their mooring place to the crumbling barns in the distance came neither sound nor motion.

With weapons in their hands, and eyes and ears alert, the crew gathered on the deck and gazed at the homesteads. Suddenly, they heard the sharp bark of a dog. The others stood tense, doubting their ears, but Captain Gunnar boomed out:

"Halloo!"

No answer came.

"Half of us will go ashore," decided Asbrand. "The others must stay to man the ship. Be wary; the Skraellings may lie in wait for us."

Vahl and Baard took their places among the men ashore. Home after home seemed empty, yet in each some of its owner's gear lay undisturbed. Around most of the cottages the stone walls had fallen down, but some were in good repair. Within one fence they even found a few scrawny cattle grazing.

"If this place is deserted," said puzzled Asbrand, "it has certainly not been so for fifty years. Where is that dog?"

"There!" cried Vahl, pointing. He had seen a shaggy brown head appear over one of the low walls. The beast scrambled up and stood growling at the strangers. With more curiosity than judgment, Vahl and Baard vaulted the wall in the opposite direction, running toward the cottage it enclosed.

"Back, back!" shouted Asbrand. "Guard yourselves!"

But no murderous Skraelling arrow winged toward them. Only a very short, very plump, very round-faced brown creature appeared in the doorway. She supported on her shoulder the weight of a crippled young Norseman, dressed, like herself, only in sealskin pantaloons.

"Are you friends?" he demanded, pale and tense.

"We are!" shouted Asbrand and the whole company, running to surround the Westerners. "We have come from the Eastern Settlement to see how you fare!"

"Welcome, kinsmen!" cried the young man joyously. To the silent woman at his side he spoke in quick, strange syllables, which she answered in the same tongue. "My mother bids you be our guests."

Using his mother as a crutch to replace his injured leg, the young man hobbled back into the house. Vahl and Baard led the group which crowded in after him. The room was so small that it scarcely held ten in comfort. Asbrand delayed outside to whisper warning to those who could not squeeze in. He bade some stand guard, others explore the village for more people, and others carry the news back to the ship that people had been found. For the time being he commanded them to keep their arms ready.

These precautions were unnecessary. Enders Erdevigsson and his mother were alone in the settlement; he, because he could not travel, and she to care for him. Some women and the young children of the homesteads were birding in nearby cliffs. The others, with the men of the settlement and the older boys, were hunting in the north for seal and bear and caribou meat to store away for the long, cold winter.

"We feared your people had all been killed by the Skraellings!" Enders was told.

"Those kindly folk? They have been our best friends!" he declared indignantly.

"How have you managed to live all these years without any goods from the Eastern Settlement?" asked Asbrand.

"The Skraellings helped us, or we would have died. They taught our people how to feed and clothe themselves from nothing but the wild creatures of the ice and how to make boats of skin. My mother," he added proudly, "is a Skraelling woman. There are now both men and women of her blood among the village families."

The men stared at the Skraelling woman. She smiled back. Her stringy black hair was oiled and twisted into a tight knot on her head; below it, her round face with its squinted black eyes was as brown as a Turk's. She squatted comfortably by a pot of fresh meat. She had set it to boil over a lighted stone lamp at the cooking place in the center of the house.

"We have brought you gifts of grain, thinking

it must be long since you have eaten bread," Asbrand told his host.

"Within my whole lifetime no one in the village has tasted it," said Enders. He thanked his visitors heartily; but when two of the men ran back to the ship and brought one of the sailors' hard-baked loaves, Enders could not hide his disappointment. Plainly he preferred his usual diet of meat. As for his mother, one bite of the flat stuff was enough for her.

But if the bread failed to please them, the spear-points and knives which the *Good Shepherd* had brought did not. Of all the things which their people had once bought from Europe, Enders said, they missed steel blades the most.

About a dozen women and twice as many children soon returned to the village, loaded with leather sacks of eggs and eider down. Some had the features of tall, thin, blond Norse folk with gray or blue eyes; others were short, plump, dark-haired, dark-eyed Skraellings with noses scarcely protruding beyond the curve of their cheeks. Most of the children were a mixture of both. Tired as they were after their long walk, they still had enough energy to talk all at once in the excitement of seeing strangers. The older women and their children still spoke Norse, but among the others, the strange words of the Skraellings were most common.

Norse or Skraelling, they welcomed their guests.

That they were blood kin, there was no doubt. Many could trace common ancestors. One old dame claimed kinship with Asbrand. A sister of his grandfather had married a man of the Western Settlement, and the woman was grandchild to that pair. In her family there had been no marriage with the Skraellings, and her ten-year-old grandson Taage spoke the clearest Norse among the children.

When the people discovered that there was a priest among their visitors, they insisted on going at once to the church for prayer and praise. Eagerly they crowded in and knelt down, but those who spoke Skraelling did not know the ritual, and even the others stumbled over their words. It was more than twenty years since their last priest had died.

When the service was over, the people crowded around Father Anselm. The old women knelt on the hard stone floor to kiss his hand; the young women brought children to him to be baptized. Many shyly offered him gifts. When he told them that he could not accept anything for himself, but that it was his duty to collect their tithes for Holy Church, the women rushed away and came back with beautiful furs of wolf and bear, which they laid at his feet.

The visitors were divided among hospitable families, and carried off to feast. Vahl returned with Asbrand and Baard to Enders' cottage. While they ate his mother's good boiled meat, talk flew fast.

Enders wanted the visitors to sail northward until they found one of the hunting parties from the Western Settlement. Asbrand, however, declared that they were in honor bound to stay only for a few days for falcon hunting, but that if the men of the Osterbygd could but earn the *Good Shepherd* for their own, they would come another year.

Lame Enders assured them that he had seen falcons often around the fiord, but he doubted whether any of the season's nestlings had yet hatched. He called in several children to see what they could tell. Most of them thought the white hawks were still sitting on their eggs, but Taage had seen one eyrie where the parent birds were carrying much food. If eyases could be found, that was the place to look.

With the child for guide, Vahl, Asbrand, Baard, and three of Asbrand's henchmen crossed the valley next day. One look at the rocky cliff which Taage pointed out showed that no one could scale the rise to the falcon's nest. For many yards the sheer face offered no foothold; then layer after layer of rock jutted out, each overhanging the one below.

"It is lucky we came well supplied with rope," said Asbrand, watching one of the birds wing away from the ledge to the sea. "If we reach the nest, it will have to be from the top of the cliff."

He bade Baard stay below, to signal to the climbers the position of the eyrie. With Taage leading, the others climbed the nearest cliff which offered a foothold. The heavy braided leather rope which Asbrand had brought was used to bind the men together, so that if one slipped the others might save him from a dangerous fall. The Greenlanders' soft boots gave them firm footing on the rocks, but Vahl's shoes slipped and slid, and his hands were soon bruised from clutching at the rough rocks. He sighed with relief when he could hoist himself onto the cliff top.

With Baard to give them their position, the Greenlanders looped one end of the rope around a huge boulder, and began to fasten the other around the waist of one of Asbrand's men.

"Surely I should go down!" protested Vahl. "I was sent here because of my knowledge of the birds."

"We are all birders," Asbrand answered. "Do not fear but that we shall do our best for you."

"That I trust fully," Vahl agreed. "But when I go back to the court of Burgundy, how can I say, 'Another man risked his life for Count John, while I watched him and did nothing'? Let me try!"

Asbrand reluctantly agreed. Vahl took off his shoes, so that his bare feet could cling to the rocks. Asbrand's men knotted the end of the rope around Vahl's body so that it formed a swinging seat. Obeying their orders, Vahl walked slowly backward over the edge of the cliff. The men lowered him as gently as they could, and Taage lay flat on the ground trying to watch him over the brink.

The wearing of the rope cracked off loose stones, which catapulted down, missing Vahl's head by a hair's breadth. The twisting of the rope threatened to batter him against a ledge, but by thrashing about he kept his face turned toward the cliff. Once he looked down at Baard, but the height made him dizzy, and the rocks below looked cruelly sharp. He hastily gazed at the wall of rock again, and watched anxiously as he neared the ledge where the two young eyases perched on their crude brush nest.

"I see them!" he shouted at last triumphantly. With a swing he pushed himself up on the ledge a few yards from them, balancing himself against the backward pull of the rope. Getting down on his knees for greater stability, he unstrapped the leathern hamper from his back and began to inch cautiously toward the young birds. They began chittering at his approach. Not yet old enough to fly, they fluttered nervously but still huddled in the nest. He saw with anxious eyes a white speck in the sky down the valley. A parent falcon was flying home to its young. That fierce bird, seeing an intruder — Vahl hurriedly picked up the longest stick near him in the nest, and managed to herd both birds toward the open hamper. One fluttered in with a final squeak, but the other struck at him with its powerful beak, and drew blood from his cheek.

Desperately he clutched at the fledgling, thrust it inside his bag, and fastened the lid with agitated fingers. The white speck in the sky was much closer now.

Binding the hamper fast on his back, he reached out to tug on the rope as a signal that he was ready to go up. His hand stopped in mid-air. Beyond his reach above him, invisible to the men on the cliff, the strands of the leather rope had worn dangerously thin; one of the thongs had snapped! And the great white bird was coming nearer.

"Give me more rope! And watch that bird!" he yelled, retreating under a rocky overhang so that the bird could not dive on him with full power. He heard the men shout in answer, saw an arrow flash toward the flying hawk. As well try to hit a streak of lightning, but the noise and motion disturbed the falcon. It veered sideward and swept off across the valley. Vahl pulled feverishly on the slackened rope, but it tightened far short of the break.

"No more rope!" Asbrand shouted down.

The falcon had turned back from the opposite cliffs and was streaking toward its eyrie. Even if Vahl could beat off its vicious beak and talons without toppling off the narrow ledge, what then?

"Pull!" he shouted desperately.

He gritted his teeth and stepped off into the dizzying emptiness of the air. Above him the rope squeaked and grated more and more loudly under the strain. He heard a snap as two leather strands broke — then another. He shut his eyes. He was sure he was falling.

"Reach up!" cried Asbrand's voice. Strong arms seized him and pulled him over the cliff edge. He staggered; his knees gave way; he fell face downward.

"What ails you?" Asbrand clapped him jovially on the shoulder, hearing the chittering from the hamper. "Surely you got the birds!"

"The rope!" stammered Vahl. "The rope!"

Asbrand and his men snatched at it. Sweat started on Asbrand's forehead, and he made the sign of the cross. Only two slender strands still held the break together.

But of the eight falcons which Vahl and Sir Olivier had come so far to find, two at least were secure.

13

Storm and Sunshine

WO DAYS LONGER the visitors stayed in the Western Settlement. Each day searching parties followed women or children who tried to guide them to other falcon nests; but in the only one they found, neither egg was hatched. It seemed best to Vahl to wait no longer, but to take the two birds he had back to the Eastern Settlement. The eyases were strong, wild creatures, not yet ready for flight. Vahl kept them on the ship, where a mews had been fitted up in the stern castle. He began to train them to the hood, and with the whistle when they fed. They throve on morsels of raw meat.

On the third day the crew of the *Good Shepherd* rowed down the long fiord toward the sea. Behind them, Enders and all the women and children of the village waved to them from the steep bank below the church, and many wept to see them go. But Taage shouted with joy, hugging to his breast the fine Italian dagger which Vahl had bought in Bruges. The child had steadfastly refused payment for finding the birds when he had learned the story of their seeking, but a parting gift of friendship he could not refuse.

In the *Good Shepherd,* all were in high spirits. The men knew their kinsfolk safe, they had lost their fear of the Skraellings, and looked forward to later visits to the good hunting lands of the north with them. The priest rejoiced in the baptisms he had performed, in the faith he had strengthened, and in the tithes he had collected. Vahl whistled merrily as he cared for the young eyases.

Captain Gunnar ordered the ship anchored for the night hours in a sheltered inlet, not caring to venture out among the ice floes until dawn. Morning brought little more light than the brief twilight of night, for the sun remained hidden behind dark clouds. An offshore breeze sprang up, filling the *Good Shepherd's* two sails and making it easy for the crew to maneuver the ship through leads in the pack ice into the open ocean.

"We shall make a quick sail home," said Asbrand happily.

Sails and oars sent the ship speeding southward, but rain began to fall. The rising wind swept great sheets of water across the deck. The rain was only the beginning of a wild storm. For five days and nights the *Good Shepherd* was borne before a mighty wind which blew steadily from Greenland over the sea. Drenched and miserable, the men bore the driving downpour as best they could. Vahl suffered less than the others, for he huddled with his birds under shelter. Even there cold and damp chilled him through.

Late on the fifth day the battered ship, with one mast broken, was driven close in to a stony shore. The men battled their way to safe harbor on the lee side of a rocky promontory where they could wait out the storm. Sheltered from the wind's fury, they crowded at the bulwarks to gaze at land which none of them had ever seen.

"See how the ledges rise wide and flat from the sea!" cried Asbrand. "This must be that Flagstone-land of which the old sagas tell!"

"God grant it!" said Captain Gunnar grimly. "Then Markland is to the south. We must find wood to mend our mast if we expect to end our days anywhere except on this barren shore."

Sunlight came and the swells died. The disabled ship sailed slowly south. There was no sign of human life along the whole forbidding coast, though seals and walrus dotted the skerries and the beaches and seabirds flew overhead. Once Vahl saw a white falcon flying out to sea and took it for a good omen. Trees, at first visible only as dark green patches far inshore, began to crowd closer to the water. After three long days, Captain Gunnar found a rocky inlet with a fringe of tall spruce trees, and there anchored to repair the mast.

"If the old stories are right," said Father Anselm, "we have only to sail a few days farther south to find Vinland!"

"I long to go on the Vinland venture," said Vahl slowly, "but my duty is to look for falcons —"

"We can make the two hunts one!" said Asbrand, as eagerly as the priest. "Come! While the mast is repaired, we can explore the coast for men and birds." But they found no sign of either. Vahl was secretly glad, for he too longed to see Vinland the Good.

But the voyage farther south lasted only one short day. The ship was caught by a strong current and crashed into a submerged rock. The ship's keel was broken. By the greatest good luck a nearby inlet offered harbor, and the ship was quickly drawn up on its sandy beach.

"This will take many days to repair," said the captain, shaking his head over the damage.

"Here ends our voyage to Vinland!" sighed Asbrand.

"Why? Why? Surely we cannot come so far and turn back?" cried Father Anselm.

Captain Gunnar let Asbrand answer. "The days are passing. Soon Greenland will be frozen in winter ice again. We must return before that happens."

The priest stared from one to the other and read bitter disappointment in both faces. "Aye — we must go back," he agreed. But his voice trembled.

"Well, let us make the best of what we have," said Captain Gunnar. "While the best craftsmen mend the keel, let the rest cut lumber to load the ship. A visit to Markland should not be wasted!"

Vahl and Baard went falcon hunting. For two days they saw no birds, but on the third their luck changed. Sitting high on a rocky ledge near the inlet, they looked down into a sea of green treetops below them. Both gasped. Over a nest in the top of a gnarled pine tree, standing gaunt and bare, flapped a pair of huge white wings.

"A falcon! Feeding young!" Vahl whispered. "Stay here and watch the nest, for fear I lose my way!" Quietly he scrambled down the side of the cliff to the wooded valley. Fallen trees blocked his way, and openings through which he could see Baard were few, but he found the tree he sought. He crouched below until the mother bird flew away. Then he climbed the rough, resinous trunk until he reached the fledglings' lofty perch of crudely woven dead twigs and branches. There were two eyases. Just as he placed the first, squawking wildly, in his bag, the parent bird returned with new-caught prey. Seeing an intruder, she shrieked and plunged toward him, dropping her burden to free her vicious talons for a strike.

Vahl ducked under a branch and saved himself from the full force of her attack, but she struck again at closer range and gashed deeply one hand which he could not snatch away quickly enough. He climbed down and cowered under the tree until the bird had grown silent. He would have liked to climb again to the nest, but the falcon stood on guard on the edge, and he dared not try.

The sun had reached the horizon; dusk would soon fall. Vahl did not care to be caught overnight in the forest. He crept out of hiding and looked for Baard on the cliff. No one was there; perhaps the falcon had attacked him, too.

Vahl spent two weary hours struggling through the dead limbs which littered the forest floor before he reached the bay shore with his falcon prize. The moon, rising clear and bright, turned sea and shore to silver, and made his path plain.

As he stumbled tiredly toward the ship, he passed two great boulders near the water's edge. On one he sat down, resting his torn hand on the cool stone. A finger entered a hole, and even at its full length felt no end. Vahl bent down to look at the opening. It was round and straight. It had been drilled the length of a man's hand through the end of the boulder which projected toward the water.

Vahl knew that while northern seamen used iron anchors on some larger vessels, it was customary for small skiffs to carry mooring stones with them; and where big boats often anchored, the sailors frequently chose a big boulder on the shore and inserted in it an iron ring or spike to which they could fasten their vessel by strong leather ropes. Here was neither ring nor spike, but such a hole in such a place had certainly been made by northern boatmen.

"An anchor stone! I have found an anchor stone!" Vahl shouted, leaping up. The sailors came tumbling over the rocks to see the first sign anyone had found that men of their own kind had been on this strange coast before.

"The ring is gone!" panted the first who came up, as he saw the empty hole.

"Maybe it rusted away. If Thorfinn Karlsefni's men used it, it has had four hundred years to disappear," said another.

"There is no sign of rust!" Vahl protested. He was disappointed at the sailor's suggestion; he wanted to find men living, not dead. Asbrand, who had come up to the group with Captain Gunnar, examined the hole in the bright moonlight and agreed with him.

"Iron was as precious to Thorfinn as to us," he reminded his men. "Whoever drilled this stone, he or another must have carried the ring on with him to another harbor. But maybe he left some other human sign behind him. As soon as the sun rises, let us all seek for one."

The whole party searched diligently for many hours the next day, but found nothing more. Reluctantly the crew went back to loading the ship with lumber. Vahl and Baard again climbed the cliff to locate the falcon's nest, but it was deserted. Parent birds and second eyas had flown. But Vahl was not much cast down. The Markland falcon was safely in the ship's mews with the two from the Western Settlement. One falcon from Markland was far better than none; at the worst, he and Sir Olivier needed only five more.

When the *Good Shepherd* put to sea again, bound for Greenland, Vahl saw Father Anselm gazing back at the forested shore with tears in his eyes. Perhaps somewhere in that limitless country stretching to the south and west, in Vinland, that beautiful land of mild winter and self-sown wheat, were the lost children of Holy Church whom he had hoped to find. But now he might never know.

14

Surprises

IX WEEKS AFTER it had sailed for the Western Settlement, the *Good Shepherd* rowed up Einarsfiord in the soft sunlight of late evening. The lookout on the rocks shouted wildly to the seamen. They could not make out his words, and waved careless greeting as they passed him by. The fishermen had evidently put up their boats for the night; the *Good Shepherd* met no one. Even when it reached the divide and turned left to White Rocks, the water stretched empty. Captain Gunnar frowned.

"Strange the *Saint Sunniva* is not anchored here."

"Oh, it has doubtless gone to Gardar," suggested Asbrand, unconcerned.

When the ship drew near White Rocks, the shouting sailors waked the echoes with their noise.

The village people came rushing down to the wharf to welcome them. Gunhilda flew straight to her father, and sobbed in his arms.

Vahl looked about for Sir Olivier, but he was not there. For a moment he wondered if the knight's hurt still kept him from walking. Then he heard Gunhilda saying through her tears:

"— and after the great storm, we gave up hope of your lives. Yet Sir Olivier waited for your return until we all feared he would be icebound here if he stayed longer. Yesterday he sailed away in the *Saint Sunniva.*"

Vahl's heart gave a painful thump in his breast. Quickly he glanced from face to face, unable to bear the terrible news, unable to believe it. But he saw Captain Gunnar and Father Anselm both standing white and still, as stunned as he. Swallowing hard, he asked huskily:

"Did he get the eight falcons?"

"Only six," sobbed Gunhilda.

Vahl's jaw dropped. "He would not — he should not! — have left if his mission was unfulfilled!"

"What else could he do?" cried Gunhilda, indignant at the anger in Vahl's tone. "When the nesting season was over, the men tried to catch grown birds with nets and pitch, and failed. The knight said he would stop in Skalholt and buy the lightest Iceland falcons he could get, to fill the number."

"At least we will not need the Iceland falcons — if I can get back to France with the birds I have," Vahl said. In spite of himself, his voice choked.

No one slept that night, while they considered what it was best to do. By morning they had made their plans. Asbrand and a Greenland crew would sail their visitors to Iceland in the *Good Shepherd*. From there they could find a ship to take them to Norway. There Vahl could perhaps overtake Sir Olivier; Captain Gunnar could recover his ship; and Father Anselm could report to the Archbishop of Nidaros. With luck the *Good Shepherd* could escape seizure by any Norwegian vessels which might cross its path. The ship would be forced to return to Greenland through dangerous ice, but the Greenlanders were willing to take the risk in order to keep the vessel.

It was three days before they could sail, though every man of Einarsfiord worked even through the few twilight hours when the sun was below the horizon. The Markland lumber was unloaded; the ship was provisioned with meat, fish, and cheese. A cage had to be built and stocked with trapped seabirds to feed the falcons on the voyage. The Gardar tithes, and the trade goods of the Osterbygd, as much as it would hold, had gone with the *Saint Sunniva*. But the tithes from the Western Settlement were left on board the *Good Shepherd,* and every bit of spare space was loaded with furs, leather, walrus ivory, oil, and whalebone, which the Greenlanders hoped to trade in Iceland.

For Vahl there was nothing to do except to care for his three falcons. Asbrand's henchman brought fresh meat to feed them. While they perched on rocks in the sun by the old mews, he lay beside them on the rich green grass, talking to Baard and Gunhilda. When their elders would spare them from work, many other young Greenlanders gathered around.

All the boys had helped in the falcon hunts for Sir Olivier, and they told Vahl how the birds were obtained. Since nesting time varied with each pair of falcons, to capture eyases shortly before flying time had been hard. The nest by the glacier had yielded two, but the next three had come from three separate nests. Sir Olivier's sixth bird was a haggard, which a young Greenlander trapped. He smeared pitch on the high rock where it perched, so that its claws would be caught and held. But as he approached, the bird snapped at him with its cruel beak, and in its fury flapped its wings until it wrenched its talons free. It turned on the man and struck at him until two of his comrades, below, feared it would knock him from the cliff. They shot at it, and brought it down with a broken wing. Sir Olivier nursed it, and hoped its wound would heal. Its captor lost much blood from his scratches, but he fared better than some other hunters.

"The pursuit of your falcons cost three broken legs, one broken arm, and many a bruise among the Greenlanders. It was not for want of trying that they failed to secure more birds!" Gunhilda told him proudly.

She and her brother talked the hours away with Vahl, about Europe to the east, and Vinland to the west; or the boys listened while Gunhilda sang songs of Greenland to the music of Sir Olivier's lute. Having taught her to play it, the knight had left it with her at parting, and it was her greatest treasure. Vahl wished that he could find something to give her that would please her half so well.

On the morning the ship was to leave, all the folk of Einarsfiord met once more at Gardar to pray in the cathedral for the safety of the voyagers. As he had at the Thing, Father Anselm celebrated High Mass in the last bishop's gorgeous vestments, brilliant in the gray church. There was another spot of color in the bare building now, for Sir Olivier had given his gold-embroidered cloak as an altar covering.

Vahl also wished to leave a gift to the cathedral. He had money, but that would do the monks no good. He remembered the reliquary around his neck, and hesitatingly asked the abbot if the church had a place for this small relic of a saint. The abbot's old hands trembled with joy as they took the case. When the cathedral was built, a special niche was left in one wall for a saint's shrine; but never had the Greenlanders been given a relic to place in it.

"We will remember you always in our prayers! In return for this great gift, may we not give you something to take with you in memory of Greenland?"

Vahl shook his head, but suddenly changed his mind. "I will long be your debtor, holy father," he said, "if you will give me a common woolen tunic and hood, such as the Greenlanders wear."

Vahl went out in his Greenland garb to bid Baard and Gunhilda goodby. They stared at him, too friendly to be critical, but a little embarrassed because they had never seen him so shabby. They had brought him as a parting gift their finest and largest seal skin. Then Vahl was glad indeed that he was ready to show himself no less generous than they. His short velvet tunic, with the silver belt from about his waist, he gave to Baard. Around Gunhilda's slim shoulders he wrapped his fur-lined cloak of garnet color, pinning it with his fine silver mantle-brooch.

"Now you are beautiful as any princess!" he told her, laughing. But Gunhilda's bright smile suddenly twisted into a sob, and she hid her weeping against her brother's shoulder. Baard choked, and could say nothing. He was not to go to Iceland, and it was his farewell to Vahl also. The boys gripped hands hard.

A shout sounded from the ship: "All on board!"

"Come along!" cried Captain Gunnar, clapping Vahl on the shoulder as he passed, and moving with him toward the boat. The priest stopped them.

"This is farewell, my comrades."

"Farewell?" growled the captain, annoyed at what he thought must be a poorly timed joke. "What are you saying?"

"I am staying here," said the priest. Vahl saw that the monks of Gardar, ranged behind him, watched him with shining faces. The captain and he stood speechless, while a smile quirked the corners of Father Anselm's grave mouth.

"Captain Gunnar," he said, holding out a thick roll of sheepskin, "you are a good man. If you have disliked me, I have at least admired you for the reason. It is true I came here as a titheman, and I beg you to deliver the tithes I have collected, and my reports on the people who paid them, to the Archbishop of Nidaros, so that he will know I have done my work. But I came here, too, as the Holy Father's messenger, to confirm Christ's people in their faith. There are members of Holy Church who fail in their duty, like the last bishop here, who deserted his people. I, too, have failed sometimes, and doubtless the Arch-Fiend will cause me to fail again. But I have power from the Pope himself to act as bishop while I am here, and here I will stay until the true bishop comes to his see."

218

"And if he never comes?" asked the captain skeptically.

"Then I will stay here until God calls me to dwell with the saints in heaven; for hell itself would be my lot if I failed to care for His straggling sheep when He has put them into my hand."

The captain stared into the priest's dark eyes for a long moment. Then he took the roll of parchment.

"I will gladly do your errand," he promised, and suddenly kneeled. "Bless me, Father, before I go."

Vahl, too, knelt down. Immediately the whole throng bent their knees and bowed their heads, while the priest lifted up his ringing voice in an old Latin prayer for wayfarers. When they rose, captain and boy both kissed Father Anselm's hand in farewell.

The ship was moving slowly from the shore when Gunhilda tore herself away from her brother and ran to the water's edge, waving wildly to Vahl.

"I beg another gift from you!" she cried. "Come back, Vahl! Come back!"

Baard, then the whole crowd, took up the cry. It was some moments before Vahl could shout across the widening space of water and be heard above the tumult:

"I will come back to you, Gunhilda! I will come back!"

Then he stood waving to his friends on shore, but though they stood in the bright sunlight, he could not see them any longer, for his eyes swam with tears.

All the voyage to Iceland Vahl kept hoping that the *Saint Sunniva* would be in port in Olafsvik when the *Good Shepherd* arrived, but she was not. More important to the Greenlanders, no other Norwegian vessel was in port either, and Vahl rejoiced with them, even though it meant his own delay.

Asbrand and his men were able to trade their cargo for iron and glass and wheat; for a good bull and boar to improve their stock; for several good wooden looms, and richly colored dyestuffs. Vahl bought a fine knife for Baard, and a silver bracelet for Gunhilda to send back with their father and his men. It was with mixed feelings of sadness and relief that Vahl and Captain Gunnar bade them good-by when the *Good Shepherd* moved out of the harbor toward the western sea. The Greenlanders were safe for awhile to enjoy their seagoing vessel.

It was well they left when they did, for two Norwegian ships came to Olafsvik a day later, and one was a man-of-war which could easily have captured the *Good Shepherd*. The other was a merchantman which made short work of its Icelandic business. Vahl and Captain Gunnar took passage aboard it back to Bergen.

Sir Olivier was still in the city. The two walked

in upon him, unannounced, while he sat at supper with Sir Anders and Dame Therese. Sir Olivier's face was turned away; he was speaking courteously to the lady, but Vahl saw that his fingers nervously twisted his great signet ring, as if his mind were elsewhere.

Captain and boy meant to surprise Sir Olivier, and they did it all too well. When the others caught sight of them and gasped, the knight turned to see the cause. He rose to his feet, clinging to the table for support. His face whitened, and he swayed.

Vahl ran to him, laughing, and set him safely in his chair. Slowly the color came back into his face, but Vahl was shocked by the lines in his thin cheeks. Sir Olivier clutched at his hands and held him close.

"Losing you so soon after I lost Artur was almost more than I could bear!" he whispered.

At the knight's tone, Vahl felt a lump come into his throat, but he managed to answer cheerfully:

"I turn up in unexpected places, and this time with three Greenland falcons instead of one."

"Thank God for that!" said Sir Olivier. "I had six, but one was injured and yesterday it died in spite of all my care. I bought three Iceland falcons in Skalholt, but they are noticeably darker and less fierce. Fortunate indeed we are to have the very number of birds we sought from Greenland."

The knight's smile faded; he put his hand to his head and slumped down in his chair.

"What ails you?" cried Vahl in panic, kneeling beside him.

"Nothing. Nothing, since you are here," Sir Olivier answered weakly.

"Never fear for him!" said Dame Therese, bustling to bring him a cup of wine. "He is but worn out. Now that he has seen you two solid ghosts, he will be a well man in no time."

She was right. Sir Olivier outdanced many a young fellow at the farewell feast Sir Enders gave for them a week later. Even Captain Gunnar swung many a partner gaily through the steps, unwilling to miss any of the jollity. Jeannette trod merrily with them both, and whispered mischievously in Sir Olivier's ear that he should note how easily broken hearts were mended, since Heinrich was there as lively as anyone, making love to a pretty cousin of Frithiof's.

Captain Gunnar left the next morning for Nidaros, to keep his promise to Father Anselm, and to beg the Archbishop on his own account to send the next bishop of Greenland to his see. Three hours later, Sir Olivier, Vahl, eight Greenland and three Iceland falcons took ship to Paris.

15

The Ransom

UNDREDS OF MILES of ocean lay between Greenland and France, and hundreds of miles of sea lay between France and Turkey, but Vahl and Sir Olivier crossed them all.

When they reached Paris, with their eleven birds still living and still healthy, Philip of Burgundy received knight and squire with feasting and gifts. One Iceland falcon he took for his own mews, one for King Charles, and one to rejoice Count John when he should come home. The eight Greenland falcons he prepared to send to Bajazet at once, and there was no one to whose care he would trust the birds except the two who had already brought them so far.

"Sir John de Chateaumorant took the first three birds safely to Turkey," he said. "And Sir

James de Helly sent back word a few days ago that the fourth falcon also reached the Sultan. We cannot risk any mischance with these."

The Duke gave his weary emissaries only three days to rest before they set out, but it was a pleasant time. All the court made much of them, but Dame Louise most of all. The Duchess and her women, when they found that knight and squire had both left their most handsome garments in Greenland, busied themselves with loom and needles to outfit them again; but Dame Louise proudly presented to each an embroidered cote-hardie of emerald velvet, already finished. When Sir Olivier recounted their adventures in the great hall, he told how Dame Louise's little reliquary had saved his life; and the whole court cheered her, while she blushed. Vahl saw that the knight spent what time he could in her company, and that when he left her it was with a jauntier spring in his step.

While the travellers were away, Sir James de Helly had made another trip between France and Turkey, completing arrangements for the ransom payment of money which Bajazet had demanded in addition to the birds. From his journey Sir James had reported one bit of news: the Duke of Milan had never sent either of his white hawks to Bajazet. One had died ("A just God's punishment of the prince!" said the Burgundians) and he was too selfish to part with the other.

Duke Philip gave a great banquet at the Hôtel d'Artois to wish Godspeed to Vahl and Sir Olivier on their journey. At its close he rose from his high seat and called on his courtiers to witness a solemn vow.

"If the worthiest knights of France return safely to their homes from the prisons of Turkey, it will be because you, Sir Olivier, and you, Vahl Thorfinnsson, have secured their ransom at peril of your lives. On the day that we welcome them here, I will give you, Sir Olivier, two hundred livres, and an equal sum every year afterward as long as you and I both live. Vahl Thorfinnsson I will make a knight with one hundred livres a year, and he shall have a high place in my household."

Vahl sat struck dumb with joy, while the Burgundians shouted and clapped. But he saw that Sir Olivier, though he tried to appear pleased, grew grave and sad. When at last they broke away from their well-wishers to snatch a few hours of sleep before leaving, Vahl asked hesitantly,

"Sir Olivier, should knighthood be for one so lowborn as I?"

The knight turned on him such flashing, angry eyes that the boy drew back. "Who questions your worth?" snapped Sir Olivier. "Name the popinjay, and I will spit him on my sword."

"There is no one," said Vahl hastily. "I saw you looked unhappy, and I feared you thought so."

"No, no!" said the knight vehemently. "My grief is purely selfish. I begrudge you to the duke. Knight you shall be; knighthood you well deserve! But I would have had you be with me, in my own household. Now I cannot ask it. Since Duke Philip has offered you a place in his court, you can rise far higher here than if you come with me."

"Whether you ask it or not," said Vahl quietly. "I will never leave you if I am welcome at your side."

The knight gazed at the boy, and smiled. He slipped an arm around Vahl's shoulders and said:

"I have a castle in the south, which I love, though even with Artur I was lonely there after his mother died. I could never bear to go back to it alone, but when John of Nevers has been ransomed, we shall go there together and rest until we recover from these weary months of battle and travel."

Vahl smiled back; then suddenly his eyes began to twinkle merrily, but he maintained a sober voice as he queried: "Would it not be well to take a good nurse with us?"

Sir Olivier stiffened, and his face crimsoned. Then he threw back his head and laughed.

"I am glad you agree! Dame Louise loves you, as I do, and I know we can all be happy together. Yet somehow I dreaded telling you that she and I planned to wed."

"There was no need," Vahl chuckled. "When your great signet left your forefinger and appeared on her hand, was not that announcement enough of a betrothal? I am glad for you both — and for myself, too!"

They embarked on a Venetian galley with a personal train of twenty richly clothed and armored men to guard them and the falcons. The ship swung around the coasts of Castile and Portugal, and began to plough swiftly through the blue Mediterranean. It was passing Sardinia when disaster struck. A sailor, carrying his oar, stumbled over a rope on the deck and fell, striking with his wooden blade the Markland falcon, weathering on its block. Down went man on top of bird, and the bird's neck was broken.

The fallen oarsman shrieked in terror, as angry men-at-arms gathered around, all in favor of hanging the luckless seaman instantly. Sir Olivier sharply bade them disperse, and sent the culprit back to his place unharmed.

"These birds were got to save men, not to slay them," he said wearily. The guardsmen retired grumbling, with such black looks at the sailor that whenever he caught one, he trembled and sweated as if he had the ague. Sir Olivier began to pace the deck, cudgeling his brain for the best remedy in a bad situation. To be almost in sight of Bajazet's dominions with the ransom, and then to be unable to deliver it, seemed to him an intolerable disgrace.

"We could stuff the skin of this poor creature, and take it to the sultan to show him we did our best. Or we could go back to France for one of the Iceland falcons," suggested Vahl miserably, turning the dead bird over and over in his hands, as if his sorrow might revive it.

"If we can do no better, we had best do both of those things," said Sir Olivier, halting his tense steps. "But what we want is another Greenland falcon, and there is one closer to us than France."

"The Duke of Milan's?" asked Vahl glumly. "There is no use thinking of that, since he will not part with it."

"I am not so sure," said Sir Olivier slowly. "I know Gian Galeazzo Visconti; I might be able to persuade him."

"Do you mean you are old friends?" asked Vahl, puzzled.

"Say rather, old enemies," said the knight grimly. "He would not give me the bird for love! I served his father in my young days in Italy. There is a streak of cruel madness in all the family, and he had his faults, but he dealt generously with me. When he died, Gian Galeazzo offered me a great sum if I would be his *condottiere*. But when he demanded that I serve him with treachery to his uncle as well as with arms, I threw his gold back in his face and found another patron. He swore that if ever afterward I entered his dominions, he would have me slain first and inquire the reason for my coming from my corpse. If I went to him, it is unlikely I would live to utter a message."

"Then tell me what to say and send me!" Vahl begged. "I will do anything to get the bird."

"Anything?" asked the knight with curious intentness. "You would be safer than I, but you would risk your life."

"I have risked it before," said Vahl impatiently.

Sir Olivier walked up and down the deck in silent thought; then he turned away, and Vahl heard him give orders for the ship's course to be charted toward Genoa.

By the time they reached the half-moon harbor of the famous port, their plans were made. Genoa had recently become French, to protect herself from conquest by the Duke of Milan, who had seized most of northern Italy. In Genoa, among friends, Sir Olivier waited, guarding the seven remaining birds. Vahl, robed, armed, and mounted like a prince, rode north alone through the Ligurian hills into the plain of Lombardy.

"Always act the haughty noble," Sir Olivier had cautioned him. "Like every upstart, the Duke is proud of his rank and scorns to deal with common men. Above all, be calm; Gian Galeazzo is a nervous coward, and the battle will be half won if he believes you are unafraid."

Vahl had expected to seek the Duke in his capital, but learned in Tortona that he was spending the autumn near Pavia, much closer. He had a small but luxurious palace five miles north of the town. Gian Galeazzo Visconti cared nothing for religion, but he was a proud patron of arts and learning, and a year before had laid the cornerstone of a great Carthusian monastery in a park near the palace. Now the Gothic nave of a magnificent church was slowly rising under his supervision.

The Duke was dining with his Duchess in his palace hall when he was told that the envoy of France to Turkey sought audience with him. When his retainers assured him that the young man had a princely bearing, and would enter unarmed, the Duke commanded that he be admitted.

Gian Galeazzo Visconti had a twisted smile which marred his face with a perpetual leer. But he welcomed the young messenger in perfect French with every sign of hospitality, had him seated at his own table and served like himself from platters of gold, heaped with an almost endless succession of rare dainties. The Lombard lord enjoyed displaying his wealth.

"I come on behalf of my father, Sir Olivier of Artois, to beg your Greenland falcon for the ransom of the French knights now prisoners of Bajazet," Vahl stated proudly when the Duke asked his business. He saw the Duke stiffen at Sir Olivier's name.

"Is your father, then, among the warriors held in Turkey?" asked the Duke. His expression made Vahl think of his nickname. His tongue played about his lips like a viper's.

"Not so," Vahl answered. "He waits for me in Genoa."

The Duke looked puzzled. "What price does he offer?"

"None but your clear conscience," replied Vahl calmly.

Gian Galeazzo laughed. His laughter sounded cold and rusty. "Why should I give my treasure to an enemy?" he asked.

"For your daughter's sake," said Vahl, nibbling delicately at a sweet olive, hoping the trembling of his hand did not show.

"How so?" asked the prince. He ceased his laughing. The lady Isabelle laid down her spoon, and held herself rigid.

"If I do not return in two days' time with the bird," Vahl explained, his tone as unconcerned as if the talk consisted of pleasantries about the delightful Italian weather, "the swiftest couriers in Genoa will be on their way to France, and the Duchess of Orleans will shortly find some of her food highly indigestible."

The Duke choked on the wine he was sipping. "The devil take you! Valentina has been in danger enough already. She may be poisoned by now for all I know! If she does come to harm, there will be war in France."

"There is more likely to be war in Lombardy," said Vahl smoothly. "In fact, French soldiers are upon your border now — with Sir Olivier in Genoa. Did you think it would please His Majesty King Charles of France, and His Grace the Duke of Burgundy, to learn that many of their noblest knights died in battle, and others now rot in prison, because it amused you to betray them to the enemy of our holy Faith? You can be sure that your daughter is alive and well, because she is their best hostage for John of Nevers and his knights. It is well known in France that if it pleased you, Bajazet would slay his prisoners. If it were not so, a French army would have been on your soil months ago. Now, if you do not give me your falcon to complete the ransom payment, Bajazet may slaughter his prisoners in any case. With their kinsmen's lives in pawn, can you doubt the French would act?"

"I can take care of myself," scoffed Gian Gale-azzo.

"Perhaps," Vahl admitted quietly. "Meanwhile your daughter will certainly pay the penalty for your misdeeds. If you wish it so, that is entirely your affair."

"Nay, it is mine, too!" the Duchess Isabelle burst out. "My lord, I would not plead with you for my nephew John; he shall be my enemy as long as he is yours. But if he must be saved to save our daughter, I pray you let it be done! My brother Philip is a vengeful man. Is a single bird worth the risk of your daughter's life, and the risk of war on your great and growing realm?"

The Duke heard her through, frowning. Then he sat silent, his fingers drumming on the table. Vahl held his breath.

"For Valentina's sake —" Gian Galeazzo began at last, and Vahl sighed with relief. But the door of the banqueting hall was flung open, and a knight strode in, resplendent in richest orange and purple velvet.

"Ah, Rinaldi!" the Duke cried, while the Duchess' lips tightened. "Our little jest is played out! I cannot have war for a single bird; so I have been persuaded at last to part with my falcon by Sir Olivier's son here."

"Sir Olivier's son?" Vahl's heart sank like a stone at the courtier's voice. Paris — Turkey — and now Italy — the same dark Italian! "I heard so and came to see!"

He stalked to the Duke's side and stared at Vahl contemptuously. Vahl stiffened and met his gaze proudly. "I smelled a rat!" the knight sneered. "Fine feathers do not make fine birds! My lord, he is an impostor!"

"Impostor?" Gian Galeazzo rose angrily to his feet.

"This knave is no son of Olivier of Artois! He is a mere lackey — the hireling falconer of John of Nevers!"

"I am foster-son to Sir Olivier!" declared Vahl with what assurance he could muster.

"No doubt — when there is gain to be made from it!" gibed the knight. "My lord, I saw him in his rags in Bajazet's camp, doomed to death. By what trick he escaped I know not. But I have come just in time to save you from more trickery!"

"Ho, there, guard!" roared Gian Galeazzo. "Drag this upstart to the dungeon! I am only sorry his so-called father did not come himself on this mission! I would make him regret it, as this trickster shall, with a slow and painful death!"

"Never fear but that Sir Olivier will come yet!" cried Vahl defiantly as two strong men-at-arms seized him and hustled him off. "And when he does, your kingdom and your daughter will be lost!"

He saw the Duchess leap to her feet, spilling her wine, as he was marched away. He tried to hold himself erect and to show no fear. But when he was pushed through a dark hole in the basement of the castle to fall sprawling in a black, measureless cavern, with rats for company, he sat on the damp stone pavement and bowed his head in his hands. Sir Olivier would come some day, truly, but too late to help him.

He never knew how long he sat there, but at

last the light of torches from above roused him. He tried to rise, to face his doom bravely, but his cramped, stiff limbs refused to lift him. Stupidly he blinked at the Duchess' face, framed in the bright rectangle of the dungeon's trap door.

"I cannot rest!" she wailed. "Prisoner, I adjure you by your faith in the Holy Cross, tell me the truth! Is Valentina in danger?"

Vahl made another effort, and this time stood erect. "Madame, I swear she will be, until John of Nevers can be ransomed."

"I will not have her suffer!" moaned the distraught Duchess. "Let down the ladder!" she bade her men. "Falconer, come quietly. I am risking much! The keeper of the white hawk waits for you in the courtyard with the bird. And lest harm should come to you or it, an armed escort will take you to Genoa. But speed! speed! before the Duke discovers what I have done!"

Overcome, Vahl knelt and kissed her hand. She tore it from his grasp, and vanished with her torchbearers. A squire led Vahl stealthily out of the castle. The bird and the promised men-at-arms were waiting in the shadows.

Out on the highway, the moon gave clear, white light. Vahl set his horse at a gallop, his heart beating easier at every clatter of the hooves.

Sir Olivier and his twenty followers, mounted on stout horses, were watching for Vahl at the north gate of Genoa when his cavalcade appeared next day. The Milanese guard rode back impressed by the foreigners' martial looks and open purses, while the French hastened to pass within the wall and through the city. Down the steep narrow streets they rode, past hovels, parks, and palaces; past the many churches with their little domes, and their façades striped in black and white marble; past the cathedral and the Doge's tower, and down to the level shore where their galley waited. With the Duke's bird safe on board, they wasted no time putting to sea again.

The new falcon, being full-grown and well trained, was the finest of all the hawks on the ship. Sir Olivier carried it on his glove hour after hour, and many a time he chuckled as he looked at it. "For once in his life Gian Galeazzo has made a slight payment for his misdeeds!" he gloated.

The bright sails of the ship billowed in a favorable wind. The travellers had but to pass through the Hellespont, and their voyage would be over.

The ship anchored at Rodosto, the nearest port to Bajazet's capital of Adrianople. The Burgundian party expected to travel overland to the Sultan's court. But in Rodosto they learned that the conqueror had gone to Bursa, which had been the capital of the Ottoman empire until his father's time.

The ship therefore sailed to the town of Mudania, across the sea of Marmora. It was a thriving little place, through which passed all the sea trade of Bursa. The governor of Mudania, on learning the travellers' errand, sent officers to escort them.

Bursa was built less than forty miles inland, on the lower slopes of a mountain so high that even at the end of the hot summer its peak was still white with snow. Between port and city stretched orchards of olive and mulberry. Bursa itself was shady with trees, and their color was echoed in the soft blue-green of the tiles which formed the most beautiful of all the minaretted mosques. Many of the tiles were used also to adorn Bajazet's palace courts, with their cool, playing fountains.

It was strange to Vahl to be received in the Sultan's palace with all the honors due a prince, when once he had been flung, covered with blood and dust, a helpless prisoner at the conqueror's feet. It was strange to speak to the monarch on his golden throne, through Vahl's captive friend, Sir James de Helly, as man to man. The Sultan knew much of falcon lore; question after question he asked and Vahl answered about the white hawks and the northern land from which they came. He begged Vahl to instruct his own falconers in the care and training of the birds. This Vahl was glad to do, to while away the days during which he and Sir Olivier had to wait for the French knights to be brought from their inland prison.

Yusuf, Ibrahim, and Ali were all glad to see Vahl again. They bore him no grudge for Mehmet's death, since Allah must have willed it. When they learned that Sir Olivier suffered from aches in the bones that had been broken in Greenland, they took both knight and squire to the Turkish bath at the hot springs nearby, so that Sir Olivier could sweat away the pain. If the Burgundians had not been feverish with impatience to see what French knights still lived, they would have gloried in the restful days. Even Sir James de Helly could not tell them who, or how many prisoners, would be delivered to them.

At last Bajazet summoned them to his presence, and the captives were led into the great hall. They were terrible to see. Their chains had been struck off, but the marks of the irons still showed on wrists and ankles. John of Nevers bore himself with wild gaiety in the excitement of release, but it was as if a skeleton laughed among the living, so cadaverous was he.

All the prisoners were scant of flesh and pale of skin and scarcely able to move their limbs from weakness. But Vahl was amazed at their number; there were nearly a hundred, far more than he had dared to hope.

"I have thrown in a few more prisoners than I promised," the Sultan yawned carelessly. "They were picked up here and there over the countryside after the battle, when my thirst for revenge was slaked. Dispose of them as you will. Your chase of these falcons deserves some reward." He stroked proudly one of the fierce birds which he carried on his gauntletted fist.

Sir Olivier bowed himself to his knees, and began to thank the ruler in his courtliest phrases. His rich voice had scarcely formed the first words before its tone was echoed from the last rank of prisoners in an ecstatic cry:

"Father!"

Sir Olivier leaped to his feet, turning toward the voice. Vahl, who had knelt beside him, stayed at the foot of the throne, staring.

Artur, thin, pale, weak, but still Artur, pushed his way through the startled Frenchmen. With his last strength he staggered toward his father, and fell fainting in the knight's arms.

"My son! My son!" murmured Sir Olivier. His voice broke, and he could say no more. He only stood there holding the boy's starved frame in his strong clasp, looking down at the white face.

Slowly Vahl rose and stood beside them. He was glad to see Artur; he was glad that Sir Olivier had found his son. Yet the bleakness of his own future rose before him. He would not lack; Duke Philip would see to that. But he had looked forward to a home. He had come to think of Sir Olivier as both father and friend. Now what need had the knight of a foster son, when his own flesh and blood was returned to him from the grave? None. None! That dream was over.

Artur's eyelids flickered. Gently his father set him on his feet, supporting him on one side while Vahl sprang to be his prop on the other.

"I was — in the cottage — when you — stole the horse —" breathed Artur to Vahl faintly, and collapsed again. This time Vahl caught him.

"My son," said Sir Olivier to Vahl, "carry your brother to our apartments. Thank God we shall soon go home together!"